# SURFER GIRL

## A Guide to the Surfing Life

### BY sanoe lake
### WITH STEVEN JARRETT

LITTLE, BROWN AND COMPANY

New York ⚭ Boston

Text copyright © 2005 by Sanoe Lake and Steven Jarrett
All rights reserved.

Little, Brown and Company

Time Warner Book Group
1271 Avenue of the Americas, New York, NY 10020
Visit our Web site at www.lb-teens.com

First Edition: May 2005

Library of Congress Cataloging-in-Publication Data
Lake, Sanoe, 1979-
   Surfer girl: a guide to the surfing life /
   by Sanoe Lake with Steven Jarrett.—1st ed.
      p. cm.
   Includes bibliographical references.
   ISBN 0-316-11015-9
1. Surfing for women—Juvenile literature.
   I. Jarrett, Steven. II. Title.
GV840.S8L34 2005
797.3'2'082—dc22  2004016161

10  9  8  7  6  5  4  3  2  1

Book design by Georgia Rucker

TWP

PRINTED IN SINGAPORE

Comics illustrations by Robert Myers
Instructional art illustrations copyright
   © 2005 by Stacy Peterson
Full color icon graphics by Michael Wang

The text was set in Avenir, and the display
   types are Diphtong and Haulnhaus.

Billabong® is a registered trademark.

# TABLE OF CONTENTS

# PART IV
# SEA HAZARDS
## 65

# PART V
# THE HERSTORY OF SURFING
## 77

# PART VI
# BOARD MEETING
## 85

# PART VII
# (YOUR NAME HERE) LEARNS TO SURF
## 95

5

# BE A SURFER, OR JUST BE LIKE ONE

Interested in learning one of the world's greatest sports?
Or do you just want to be part of a cool culture that,
after several thousand years of percolating, has finally
started to break into the mainstream?
    Either way, here's the place to get your feet wet.

Every section of this book provides information that's helpful for you to know about surfing — if it's not directly related to riding a wave, then it's something like the history of surfing, outfitting, fitness, surf etiquette, surf lingo, and ocean knowledge — things that cause the molecules of your body to slowly but surely start changing into Surfer Molecules. Becoming a surfer isn't just learning how to stand up on a board. . . .

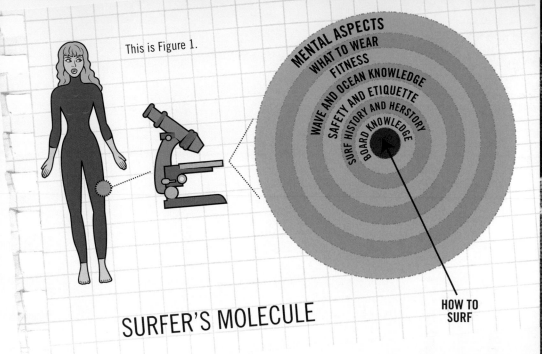

This is Figure 1.

**SURFER'S MOLECULE**

MENTAL ASPECTS
WHAT TO WEAR
FITNESS
WAVE AND OCEAN KNOWLEDGE
SAFETY AND ETIQUETTE
SURF HISTORY AND HERSTORY
BOARD KNOWLEDGE

**HOW TO SURF**

. . . And learning to surf isn't just grabbing the nearest board and going at it without any instruction or preparation. There is a proven process to learning how to surf, and right here — my little studettes — I'm going to show you how, step by step. Use this book as a reference book: read, surf, read, surf, then read and surf some more. As the concepts sink in, you'll be better able to apply them when you're on the water and there isn't time to think. That will help you stay safe, which is my number one goal. You might get a little banged up at first — you know what they say, "No pain, no gain" — but I believe a good surf guide can at least *help* prevent some nasty hits. And taking surfing lessons is an even bigger plus.

My number two goal is to build respectful surfers. Hey, I know girls are *naturally* respectful, but there are so many new people in the water these days, it's actually feeling crowded. This isn't basketball, where there's always another court to play on. In surfing, there's a finite number of breaks and waves. With more people attempting to ride those waves, it's critical to learn the basic rules of surfing — if you don't, collisions, injuries, and even worse, a lot of insults, could result.

**WARNING !**

Not that I'm trying to *scare* you or anything, but surfing is a contact sport and there is some danger. If you have any medical conditions or are taking medication, check with your doctor first. You need to be a good swimmer in the *ocean* before you begin, too. On the next page, you'll read about my mom surfing while she was pregnant with me—but she was an expert surfer long before that! To be extra safe, I'd say don't surf while you're pregnant. And finally, be especially careful with little kids in or near the ocean.

## SURF BEFORE BIRTH

My mother boogie-boarded while she was pregnant with me until she hit the five-month mark, but I didn't get on a surfboard until the ripe old age of two. That means I went two years with no surfing: by far the most I've ever spent or ever will spend, God willing, not riding waves.

My first experience on a board was on the nose of my Dad's. He'd ride behind me, steering. At five I started surfing on my own, and finally, when I was ten, the bug really bit and I began surfing practically every day.

It's not like that was unusual. I'm from Kauai, where almost everyone surfs — and if they don't surf, there's a good chance they boogie-board, swim, windsurf, or canoe. At the end of the school day I'd stare at the clock and wait for the bell — if there were waves, homework would probably wait until after dark.

It's easy for this lifestyle to follow you into adulthood. In my family, it did for sure: my mom, Laola, was a competitive surfer — she won the U.S. Surf Championship in 1976 — and my grandma swam open ocean races. Both of them, along with my dad, still surf and swim.

My great-grandmother and great-great-grandmother were also competitive waterwomen. In fact, there's an ancient tradition of women surfers in Hawaii; girls and women surfed in equal numbers — and with similar ability — to boys and men.

The sooner we get back to that, the better, don't you think?

Yeah, it's true, I had a lot of advantages in learning to surf. But I've also seen girls from all over the world succeed, whether they start at age three or sixty-three. You can succeed too, and once you catch the surfing buzz, you'll get hooked just like I did. Surfing very quickly becomes more than a sport: it's an obsession. It's pure joy. Out on the water, it might be hot and sunny or cold and storming; I don't care, it's all beautiful, and I enjoy it for what it is. I love surfing because you can make it your own: your own form of self-expression.

Three generations of waterwomen: with Grandma and Mom

Surfing is a challenge. Every day is different and every wave is a new experience. There aren't too many other sports that allow such simultaneous beauty, grace, and power. I think this is why the sport appeals to girls so much. It's peaceful, and at the same time it's an incredible adrenaline rush — surfers move *fast* out there.

Surfing makes me feel strong and confident but also vulnerable and humble. It teaches me patience but makes me all the more ambitious. It shows me that I must seize the moment, yet it always allows me another chance.

I can vent, I can relax, and I can release my stress. I can get away. Surfing is an opportunity to surround yourself with things that aren't manmade and connect with nature. Fish will fly up out of the water, seagulls will dive-bomb just outside of your reach, and if you're real lucky, dolphins might surf right along side of you. I've seen whales while surfing and it doesn't get much sweeter.

Spend some time surfing, and the ocean will start to get into your blood. Connect with nature like this and you'll start to understand why surfing is so spiritual.

And finally, surfing is about friendship. I absolutely love my surfer girlfriends. We have common interests and share a special bond — which seems especially strong when we push each other and share thrills in the water. I have so many great memories of my girlfriends, in and out of the water.

Get ready to create some of your own.

Love,

Sanoe

11/3/02
2nd day here.
Never been so content
with having nothing
2 do. I love it here
Surfed Cloudbreak, a little
overhead & blown to pieces,
FuN none the less. Tavarua is
insanely beautiful. Being
here is the most uneventful
life altering experience.
The Lord whispers in the
subtle breeze & SCREAMS
of His glories in the
SUNSETS

With a friend and my little bro, Kalaea

With my friends Daize and V.K.

Does sink surfing count?

If there's at least one thing
I've learned in my
life··· EGO ROBS us ALL

PART 1

# GETTING MENTAL

# 1. EMPOWER THIS

Of course the reason to surf is because it's fun, but don't be surprised when your leap into the world of surfing becomes a character-building exercise as well.

I'm starting with this subject because the mental aspects of any sport are key, and for surfing, they're beyond key: they're a part of the high that hooks so many people into the sport, and they're essential for maximizing your safety.

As you develop traits like courage, perseverance, discipline, focus, and respect, you'll find opportunities to apply them in your life on dry land: in relationships, jobs, and intellectual and spiritual pursuits, to name a few. The word "empowerment" is thrown around a lot these days, but it definitely is real — if you make it real — in surfing.

## HEART OF A LIONESS

I'm not saying I'm Miss Brave, but there's no doubt that anyone getting off the sand and entering the wilderness of the ocean has to have some courage. Does this mean that someone who doesn't feel courageous can't surf? Absolutely not. Everyone has the kind of courage it takes to surf. It's just a matter of finding it and tapping into it.

How?

The hurdles you have to clear to become a surfer include a little physical contact, a little danger, a little risk. Not too much risk if you learn the right way, but there's risk nonetheless. It takes time and getting thrown around a bit to learn how the ocean works. Overcoming these things takes staring down your fears.

Not that it's bad to be afraid — in fact, it's healthy.

I've been afraid in the water about a million times. When I was fifteen, I went out alone once at Sunset Beach as the waves were building to at least fourteen-foot faces. Dumb move. The current was too strong, my board was too small, and I couldn't paddle into the waves to catch them. After two hours and zero success, I was getting too tired to paddle. Oh, and it was getting dark too, which was creepy. It was bad planning to get stuck in the dark, and it's a bad idea to surf alone, no matter what time of day. I recommend not doing either.

    I finally mustered up the energy to paddle toward shore, which was no treat because it meant I was going into the *impact zone,* which is the area where the waves crash. It's dangerous there when the waves are that big, but I felt it was my best chance. I was operating on instinct. I got hammered and held under, but eventually I made it to shore. I was terrified the whole time, but I didn't panic — and I felt pretty good about myself for that.

    You won't be messing around with big waves, but your feeling of achievement will not be any less when you bust through the fears that you'll likely have as a beginner.

    Of course, this kind of feeling can apply to your life on dry land. If I were to tell you that when I face a tough moment, I stop and channel my "ocean courage," it would sound pretty psycho. But in a way, it's true — courage you develop from surfing will help you feel more confident in general, and that can carry over into everything.

# PERSEVERANCE (OR, HOW TO BE A SURFINATOR)

I've seen a lot of beginners hit the wall, get frustrated, and stop. You'll be making . . .

As I was saying, you'll be making a series of progressions when you learn to surf — from building your paddling strength to riding the white-water mush to riding breaking waves — and working through these progressions takes perseverance.

Once you've gutted your way through and started riding waves, you'll know darn well you can travel a difficult road to achieve an important goal — like working your way through college, for example. There's a muscle memory that will come into play whenever you see the light at the end of the tunnel and you're not sure if you can make it. You can.

## DISCIPLINE

Perseverance isn't enough. Add discipline, and now you're on your way. It's one thing to have the drive to stay with surfing; it's another to have the discipline to get out *often.* Surfing is like playing a musical instrument: practice every day and you'll learn a lot faster. If you don't live near a beach, you can still train for surfing (see Section 5). When you finally make the trip to the ocean, try to get as many days consecutively in the water as possible.

Of course, discipline is an issue only in the beginning, because after you've taken a few of the lumps, surfing is so fun that it becomes less about discipline and more about how you fit in the rest of your life after the day's surf session.

Discipline means sticking to a plan, and that means first you have to create one. There's a plan here to teach you to surf, but you might also create a plan from this book to achieve something on dry land. I like the "job interview" example. You'll need the discipline to check off the "to do's," like researching the company, the industry, and maybe even the person who'll be interviewing you. Nothing's guaranteed, but you'll usually increase your chances for success if you act in disciplined way.

## FOCUS AND RESPECT

From the shore, surfing might look deceivingly calm and organized. Out in the middle of the water, however, it can be chaotic and frenzied. When the waves are coming big and fast, and there are a lot of people out, there's a low margin for error and no room for inattention. You have to focus.

On the water, I'd say I focus well. On land, I'm sometimes scattered, but I pull it together when I need to. For example, it's not unusual for actors to have many auditions or meetings before they get a role. It's a good time to focus. When you're in your interview, you need to be listening to your interviewer. Hesitation or stumbling usually isn't favorable on land or in the water. Surfing can help because it does get you in the habit of tight focus. Click it on, and watch how people respond.

LIKE PARTYING!

Control Freaks Beware!

While focus is internal, respect is external — it's something you give. You'll respect other surfers and you'll respect the ocean. You don't beat or conquer the ocean; at best, you work with it and harness its energy for a moment. Its power is practically infinite, while yours is minimal. Small waves — two- or three-footers — can be dangerous. Life-threatening conditions can pop up out of nowhere. Control freaks beware! You better get used to *not* being the one in charge.

You can apply your respect for nature to respecting any authority figure: your parents, a teacher, a boss. Practice it and you can avoid a lot of unnecessary conflict.

◎ ◎ ◎ ◎

Now I'm not saying surfing will create great or superior people *(much)*, but I can speak for myself in saying that it has helped my confidence. And when it comes to empowerment, I do think it stacks up well against other activities (see the hard, scientific proof below).

**Figure 2.** Lake Empowerment Comparison Grid*

| CHARACTER-BUILDING QUALITY | Worrying | Eating Chocolate | Shopping | Dating | Surfing |
|---|---|---|---|---|---|
| Courage | | | | ✔ | ✔ |
| Persistence | | | | ✔ | ✔ |
| Focus | ✔ | | ✔ | | ✔ |
| Discipline | | ✔ | ✔ | | ✔ |
| Respect | | | | | ✔ |

*ACTIVITY*

*The Lake Empowerment Comparison Grid is a copyright of Lake-Jarrett Industries. Duplication, distribution, verbal utterance, or telepathic transmission is strictly prohibited unless granted by express written permission. Thank you.

All that and outrageous fun!

Now that you're revved up to enter the surfer's world, what would be a better way than to learn about how the whole thing got started?

*This is my friend, Daize Shayne. She'll be making a guest appearance later in the book, too. She has a secret to share with you, so read on.*

# 2. HOW TO KNOW MORE ABOUT SURFING THAN YOUR AVERAGE ROOKIE 101

Most surfers know little about where and when surfing began.

AN ISLAND.

A SUPER LONG TIME AGO.

It's too bad, because the history of surfing is an exhilarating story, filled with adventure, bravery, romance, cruelty, death, and rebirth . . . almost as good as your typical television dating show. Time to understand how you can be part of ancient traditions that continue to this day.

## ACT I.

### THE CALL TO ADVENTURE

As best as anyone can tell, the first wave riding was done around four thousand years ago, well before *The O.C.* hit the airwaves, by the original brave souls who left Southeast Asia in *open canoes* to explore the Pacific. The extent of their surfing was likely on body-board-style wooden planks in small surf near the shore.

The ocean travelers brought the sport to Western Polynesia, where it seems wave riding was primarily the pastime of boys. This suggests, clearly, that the sport was in its infancy.

Hawai'i

Samoa
Tonga

Marquesas
Tahiti  Tuamotus
Cooks    Australs

Aotearoa
(New Zealand)

Rapu Nu
(Easter Island)

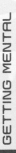

SURF BATHING

When Eastern Polynesia was colonized by the Asians and Pacific Islanders — around two thousand years ago — surfing began to be enjoyed by both sexes (and all ages).

B.C. is about to become A.D., and *girls are finally getting wet!*

Surfing also developed independently in ancient times in West Africa. It consisted mainly of children body-boarding on planks. In northern Peru, fishermen surfed waves on reed bundles, which were called *caballitos,* or "little horses." By the way, here's a picture of me and my favorite little horse.

# ACT II. THE ECSTASY AND THE AGONY

The Polynesians arrived in Hawaii around 400 A.D., and their maniacally perilous journey was rewarded with the discovery of a treasure: delicious and monstrous surf. They took the sport to heart and, over several hundred years, the Hawaiians made bigger boards and refined their shape to adapt to the larger waves. They also refined surfing techniques: they started cutting diagonally across the waves — *lala* in Hawaiian. Once you have lala, you have a whole new way to ride waves and deal with different kinds of breaks.

We have a good idea of what ancient surfing looked like then because the first Europeans to arrive — Captain Cook's sailing party in 1778 — took meticulous notes of their observations. Cook's lieutenant, James King, wrote this:

> Their first object is to place themselves on the summit of the largest surge, by which they are driven with amazing rapidity toward shore — The boldness and address with which I saw them form these difficult and dangerous maneuvers was altogether astonishing and is scarcely to be believed.

Sounds like some serious early shredding to me.

Oh, and here's the important part: women were noted as riding in numbers equal to the men and they were similarly skilled. Those were my ancestors.

Surfing evolved into something beyond just a sport in Hawaii; it was a lifestyle. Entire communities would frequently stop everything — farming, fishing, clothes making, etc. — and go surf together. It became woven into all aspects of daily life. Here's a little chart:

**Religion**      Prayers were said when a tree was cut to make a board. Strength-enhancing chants were offered to the gods by surfers before paddling out. Temples were built next to surf spots where surfers went to pray for good surf.

**High Society**  Since the Ali'i — the "chiefly class" — were relieved of everyday chores, they had more time to do what was important: surf. They kept a chanter handy that delivered a personal surf chant proclaiming their glory and skill. (Who wouldn't want one of those?) Some breaks were reserved just for the royals, and God help a surfer if he surfed the same wave as a female royal: he could be put to death for such an act.

*Keep this in mind, boys: all girls are princesses or queens in their own way.*

**Romance**       Frolicking on the water was not uncommon, and legend has it that riding the same wave as a member of the opposite sex could allow certain romantic liberties to be taken. Use your imagination.

**Festivals**     An annual celebration that lasted from October to February called Makahiki included many games and featured surfing. (A four-month party? Ah, the good old days.)

**Competition**   The Hawaiians frequently competed on the waves. One competition had a sledder on a hill and a surfer on a wave taking off at the same time and racing to a spot on the beach. (Sign me up for that.) Gambling on competitions was the norm and it wasn't unusual for someone to stake property, freedom, or even his life on the outcome. (Sign me out for that.)

This surfing "ecstasy" lasted for a thousand years — until the discovery of the islands by Europeans. Here's where our story turns to "the agony."

The arriving explorers and missionaries had huge ships and wondrous technology (like guns), and they used these wares to convince Hawaiians that their way of life and religion was superior. A cultural overthrow had begun, and by the 1820s, the Hawaiians had accepted the new religion. The Makahiki festival was ended, thus eliminating a prime fueler for sports enthusiasm, including surfing. New leisure activities — like horseback riding and card-playing — also diverted Hawaiians from surfing. Yeah, *card playing*. **Strike 1 against surfing.**

During the 1830s, a strict group of missionaries — the Calvinists — took power and actively discouraged surfing. They believed that anything that didn't involve worshipping or working wasn't worth doing, and that included water sports. **Strike 2 against surfing.**

Other missionaries simply didn't like the minimal attire, gambling, and romantic freedom aspects of surfing. Is it a big surprise that once a lot of the fun of surfing was sucked out of surfing, the Hawaiians lost a lot of interest in doing it? **Strike 3 against surfing. But wait, there's more.**

The westerners also brought diseases the natives had no immunity against. Small pox, measles, and an assortment of venereal diseases killed or sterilized many. Between 1779 and the 1890s, the population of Hawaiians decreased from about 400,000 to 40,000. That's a 90 percent decrease for those of you scoring at home. A large number of those people were, or would have been, surfers, so it wouldn't be unfair to call this a surfers' genocide. **Strike 4 against surfing.**

With the help of strikes 1 through 4, surfing in Hawaii was on life-support as the nineteenth century closed out. It was confined to Waikiki and was back to a rudimentary state: small boards on small waves ridden straight in toward the shore. At least there was some surfing going on, though. In other parts of Polynesia, in Tahiti and New Zealand for example, surfing essentially died.

But while surfing was on a respirator in Hawaii, there *was* breath, and where there's breath, there's life, and certainly the possibility for more life.

Duke Kahanamoku

22

DUKE

# ACT III. THE REBIRTH

In the early 1900s things started picking up: Honolulu residents and local schoolboys started hitting the waves in increasing numbers at Waikiki. One of the best local surfers, George Freeth, made his first trip to Southern California in 1907 and jump-started the sport there by wowing onlookers at spots like Santa Monica and Corona Del Mar.

That same year, Alexander Hume Ford, a one-man surfing promotion machine, taught author Jack London how to surf. London then wrote an article called "The Royal Sport," which appeared in a national magazine and one of his books. The surfing flame was fanned.

Surfing promoters formed the Outrigger Canoe Club in 1908, the world's first organization dedicated to promoting surfing.

THEY PROMOTED CANOEING, TOO!

By Christmas of that year, a surf contest was held in Waikiki and was won by a fourteen-year-old who rode a wave in standing on his head. The fun was back! From there, surfing took off fast. The Hui Nalu was formed (a surf club that promoted the sport specifically among Hawaiians), board shapes were refined, and Duke Kahanamoku — the grandfather of modern surfing — began working his magic on surf-watchers in Hawaii and on the mainland. By the time Jack London returned to Honolulu in 1915, surfers were working the waves with lala . . . yep, real shredding had returned to Hawaii.

It's great when stories come full circle and have a happy ending, isn't it? Well, it gets even happier; you know why?

We'll continue the story with the *her*story of surfing a little later. Next, though, since we touched on the old religious aspects of surfing, we'll turn to what is essentially a religious experience specific to the modern girl surfer: picking out something to wear.

Because girls are about to get into the mix again, that's why.

*Having Fun—
Wish you were here!*

# PART II
# YOU'VE GOT THE LOOK

# 3. OUTFITTING I:
## HOW NOT TO FLOP
## OUT OF YOUR TOP
## (AND OTHER FUNCTIONAL
## SURFWEAR TIPS)

It's a wonderful feeling to have the ocean rushing against your body. Many surfers, including me, try to enhance the experience by wearing as little as conditions allow.

Unfortunately, there's always the issue of water temperature to take into account. 68 degrees or higher usually allows for comfortable surfing without a wetsuit. There are many different types of surfwear for girls that are functional and still can look hot. Let's start with the least amount of clothing and move to the most.

## BIRTHDAY SUIT

It's legal in some places. If you're over 18 and *that* uninhibited (I'm not), feel free to find these beaches and have at it. Channel the ancient Hawaiians! Liberal use of sunblock is suggested. If you're under 18, I hereby absolve myself of legal and — more importantly — *parental* repercussions.

# BIKINIS
## Staying in Your Bikini

No scientist has accurately determined the g-force on a breast while a girl is popping up onto her board. The precise force of the water gushing across her chest also remains unknown. Let us simply say that the energy is significant in both cases, and certainly enough to cause the aforementioned breast to escape from its constraint. To prevent the mortification that would follow, check off the following:

Some evil boys may want to remove this section. For the sake of keeping the book looking neat, we're providing a dotted line; so boys, please use it.

### Preparation

If your top requires tying, take extra care to tie it properly. Knot it or bow it, whichever you prefer, but make sure to check and re-check. Clips secure? Okay, ready to go.

### Make a Smart Purchase Decision

Make sure your top fits snugly. If it's loose on shore, it's going to be much looser in the ocean because suits stretch when they get wet. Avoid bandeau tops without straps and be cautious of string bikinis with cups that slide. Sports bra–style swimsuit tops and fixed halter tops are an excellent way to go — they're usually quite secure. Sturdy cross-hatching on the part of the top that connects the cups is also helpful.

### Monitor the Situation

Not that you don't already do it constantly, but look down periodically while you're in the water to make sure you're all strapped in. Not while you're riding a wave, of course! If you feel something come loose while being churned after a wipeout, do not let this supercede using your arms and hands to protect your head as you surface. Remember your priorities: protect brains and face first; restore loose body parts to swimsuit second.

# Other Surfing-Bikini Basics

## Coverage

Bikinis that don't work so well for surfing include tiny teardrops, micros, minis, miniminis, minimicros, and severe floss-thongers. If you try to surf in them, you'll have a decent chance of ending up surfing just like the ancient Hawaiians did.

## Bruise Aversion

Avoid beads, rings, decorative knots, tassels, and tops that tie in the front — they might bruise you when you press against your board. Test halter tops for comfort by leaning your head way back and seeing if it bothers the back of your neck. When you surf, you'll be arching your neck a lot.

## Bottoms

Make sure your bottoms also fit tightly on dry land; the ocean will encourage them to slide around. I almost had a disaster once: I was surfing off Rocky Point in Hawaii when I got pounded by a big wave and my bottoms came all the way off. Fifty photographers were shooting the surfers. I freaked out underwater, but when I surfaced, I noticed that the bottoms had gone down my leg and were saved by my leash. Yippee!

Good bottoms for surfing include hipster, boy, and flex shorts. Board shorts are made for women too (they have shorter crotches) and come in short, medium, and long leg lengths.

Michelle, Kate, and me on the set of Blue Crush

28

# RASH GUARDS

Rash guards were created to wear under wetsuits to prevent chafing, but I love to wear them without wetsuits. They not only keep you from flopping out of your bikini top, they protect you from the sun and prevent your chest and stomach from getting irritated from the gritty combination of sand and wax on your board.

Rash guards are durable — they're made of nylon and Lycra — and come in various styles and colors, so it should be pretty easy to find one you like. You can get them in long sleeves, short sleeves, and tank tops. Seek out the ones with UV protection. In a pinch, you can use a t-shirt — it may not give much UV protection, but it's better than nothing.

# WETSUITS

There are no hard and fast rules about when to put on your superhero suit. If you wouldn't surf otherwise because the water is too cold, or you just want to be extra warm, that's when you put it on.

A wetsuit keeps you warm by allowing a thin layer of water to form between you and the suit, which your body quickly warms up. The side benefits of a wetsuit are: 1) sun protection — there's less exposed skin you need to apply sunblock to; 2) scrape protection: you'll avoid a few cuts and bruises; and 3) the opportunity to go as Catwoman to Halloween parties.

### Thickness

Thicker suits are for colder conditions. The two most commonly used are the 3/2 (pronounced "three two"), which is sufficient for most cool water, and the 4/3, which is used by surfers in frigid spots. The numbers refer to millimeters; the first number is the torso thickness and the second is the thickness of the arms and legs. For extremely cold water, there are suits thicker than 4/3.

A lot of surfers know that Jack O'Neill was a wet suit innovator in the early 1950s in San Francisco, but they don't necessarily know the rest of the story: It was invention by necessity, as O'Neill was looking for a way to stop the cold water from a) keeping his surf sessions short; and b) freezing his, uh, buttocks off. He helped produce six children after developing a workable suit, so it's fair to say his, uh, buttocks didn't freeze off. Eight million design changes later, we have wetsuits for every kind of body type and all kinds of conditions.

The wetsuit thickness you choose is dependent on where you surf and your tolerance for cold. You should wear the minimum you can stay warm in, because the thicker the suit, the less flexibility you'll have.

## Coverage

There used to be two basic wetsuit models: full suits (suits that covered your arms and legs) and spring suits (suits that had short sleeves and were cut above the knees). Now, coverage options are expanding by the day as manufacturers mix and match long, short, and tank sleeves with long and short legs. Let us not forget our friends the jackets: they come in short, long, or tank.

If you have just enough cash to buy one suit, I'd recommend a full suit.

## Wetsuit Purchasing Basics

A decent wetsuit will run you about $150 minimum, and they go up to $350 or more. Like most things, you get what you pay for. Cheap suits fall apart faster, keep you less warm, and are more likely to cause skin irritation. I recommend getting the best suit you can afford.

**Fit.** The suit should be very snug (but non-chafing) yet still allow comfort and flexibility. It can't be loose; if it is, there will be room for cold water to surge into the suit each time you "eat it." Misery will follow. If you can't find something off the rack that fits properly, ask the surf shop to point you to a custom wetsuit maker.

**Seams.** Check the seams to make sure they're smooth and at least appear watertight. Move your arms to make sure there's no pinching and that your movement is not restricted.

**Key Pocket.** Car-key pockets are a great idea, but most are flimsy fold-over numbers that don't feel like they'll keep the key in. See Section 7 — Gear Care — for options on managing your car key while you surf.

## Wetsuit Care

Rinse your wetsuit off thoroughly — both inside and out — after each use. If you don't, it will get stinky and itchy. To dry, lay it outside on something non-metallic or fold it over a plastic or wooden hanger. If you turn it inside out, the insides will dry faster. It's best not to hang wet wetsuits by the shoulders — they'll stretch.

## On and Off Procedure

The wrist and ankle bands of a wetsuit fit extremely tight, so don't try to pull your suit on and off like it's cotton or linen — you could end up with a hernia. Instead, scrunch up or roll down the legs and use your hands to widen the hole before shoving your foot through. Shimmy the suit up over your legs and hips, then repeat for your arms. Wear a bikini under your wetsuit. When removing the suit, roll it off.

Consider practicing this a couple of times before you do it in front of other surfers.

# SURFER'S CHANGE

When you arrive at a surf location, there might not be a bathroom available to change in, and even if there is, you might not be interested in using it because a) it might be too far away; or b) it might be *disgusting* in there.

Thank God for the Surfers' Change, the time-honored procedure for getting into and out of your surf gear in full public view. There's something extremely cool about this stealthy operation. If you're shy and nervous about the remote chance that a little skin will flash, well, remember, part of becoming a surfer is developing your courage. In no time at all, the Surfer's Change will be smooth as silk for you.

### Ingredients

✔ Wetsuit

✔ Large beach towel

✔ Bikini

✔ Ability to balance on one foot like a Romanian gymnast

### Procedure

1. If you didn't remember to leave your jewelry at home, take it off and hide it. Any jewelry you wear into the ocean will likely end up being a gift to the ocean.

2. Open car door and position yourself on the side of the door where the least number of people can see you.

3. Wrap towel around your waist, tightly.

4. Get into your bikini bottoms.

5. Remove towel and casually toss into car.

6. Put your bikini top on underneath your t-shirt. That procedure is way too top-secret to reveal in this book.

7. Toss t-shirt into car.

8. Pull your wetsuit on.

During any part of the operation, feel free to lean against the car (not the car door). You want to avoid tumbling to the asphalt. If that happens, any cuts or scrapes that you receive should be nonchalantly referred to later as a "surfing accident," and the subject should be quickly changed.

# 4. OUTFITTING II:
## DON'T RATION
## THE FASHION

## THE BODY IMAGE OF A TRUE PRINCESS

Okay, my surf princesses, I know how shopping for swimwear can be discouraging and anxiety provoking. Looking at yourself in cheap mirrors under the harsh fluorescent lights of those dressing rooms can cause you to body-bash. "I should lose/gain weight; my stomach should be more toned — look how it sticks out; I should not have eaten that cookie with lunch; my butt should be smaller; If only I were in better shape I would look good in this suit; I should be skinny enough to be able to wear something like this," and on and on we go.

I'd like to encourage you to not "should" on yourself.

Who says you're not beautiful and perfect just as you are? Hmm? Our culture? Our media? Are you going to give them that much power? I say . . . if they want a Barbie doll, then they should go buy one. They're usually on sale at Kmart. As for you, I'd like you to challenge yourself by accepting your God-given body as beautiful and perfect just as it is. You're not a puppet, are you? So don't act like one by allowing others' standards (which are usually ridiculous anyway) to control how you feel about your body.

I know about this because I've been there, done that. I've done my share of body bashing and it's a huge waste of energy.

I realize that overcoming these issues isn't easy. Our culture is so obsessed with weight. But women come in all different shapes and sizes, and that's a glorious fact. How boring would it be if we all had the same type of body?

I personally think there is nothing sexier that a woman who is comfortable in her own skin . . . regardless of her shape or size. You are too, just as you are.

It's all right to stay in shape and work out, but do it for yourself.

# BIKINI STYLIN'

As you can tell by what I wrote above, I really couldn't care if you threw away any fashion tip and just wore any bikini that pleases you. That's fine! If you're interested in tips, though, there are ways to maximize your style whether you surf in your bikini or not. I went to Billabong's lead swimwear designer, Mandy Robinson, to get some suggestions.

## Match Your Personality

Surf girls just wanna have fun, and their suits should show it. Mix and match colors and prints — try a printed top and a solid bottom. You could even try layering one bikini top over another. Halter tops are great — they give a lot of lift and shape. I also like low-rider bottoms, but make sure they're snug. Try boy bottoms if you want a little more coverage. You might look for interesting fabrics, too. You'll find them matching sportswear trends, like stretch corduroy, mesh, and simulated denim. Why not texturize?

## Skin and Hair Color

If you have light skin and hair, dark suits can work well. If your skin and hair are dark, play with bright colors: try orange or pink. If you have red hair, green suits probably aren't best, unless you're planning to be Santa's little helper. Use your regular wardrobe as a guide: if you can't imagine wearing a certain color or print away from the beach, avoid it in a swimsuit.

## Equalizing Proportions

Curvy? Play it up! Select a dark suit with extra seams for shape and consider vertical stripes. High-cut bottoms make your legs look longer. Sheer wraps and sarongs are great for sexy curves. Small breasts? Cups and/or underwires help you look larger on top, as do triangle tops, and tops with horizontal striping. Top heavy? Try a halter top with wider straps for support. Look for a low bottom with wide sides to create a balance. Very thin? Stay away from dark colors, they usually make you look thinner.

Remember, these tips are geared toward flattering you in a traditional way. Don't take them too seriously.

## BIKINI-PURCHASING HINTS

A good-quality bikini will run you $70 on up. Seems expensive, I know, but fabric costs are surprisingly high, as are the cost of cups and elastic. Stores like Target often carry last year's models of top-quality brands at around half price.

1. Don't wait until the last minute. It can take you a couple of trips to several stores before you actually find a suit you like.

2. Mentally prepare yourself for the unflattering conditions you'll find in dressing rooms.

3. Don't feel like you need to stick to one size. Sizes vary a lot among manufacturers and are not always the same size you would buy in clothes.

4. Be open to trying new styles. What looks good in a magazine may not be right for you.

## SWIMSUIT CARE:
## HOW NOT TO TRASH YOUR BIKINI

You've just invested in a hot little piece of fashion, so let's make it last.

1. Hand wash, cold water, mild detergent.

2. Hang dry, but not in direct sunlight or in view of male neighbors, unless you want to drive them insane. Dryers and direct sun fade suits and make them deteriorate faster (they break down the elastic and Lycra).

3. Read the tags: some swimsuits need to stay out of hot tubs because chlorine might ruin or fade them. What this means is that if a guy tells you that you don't need your bikini in the hot tub, he might be technically correct, which is really annoying.

Feel free to clip #3 above and put it in a safe place. Guys do not need to read it.

## AH, WOMANHOOD

Two tender subjects come to mind relative to bikinis. The first is that it is memorably unappealing to be untidy in the personal grooming area. 'Nuf said. There are many products available to manage this situation, from razors to crèmes to Brazilian bikini-waxing/torture treatments.

The second involves that time of the month — you know, the "visit from your special friend." The answer is yes, you can surf while menstruating (caveat: see section 13, The Shark Section). You can wear a bikini, too, although this story about a friend of mine might have you thinking twice:

"Diana" (name changed to protect the guilty) arrived at my towel on a crowded beach in Hawaii with the cutest white bikini on. She looked beautiful and was as happy as the day was sunny. Her only problem was the string from her tampon hanging halfway down her leg (okay, slight exaggeration). She turned three shades of sunburn red and went two shades further when I asked her how far she had walked, and she said, "All the way down the beach" — a solid half mile.

While surfing, the churn could knock that string out, so while menstruating, consider board shorts over your bikini bottom. (P.S. White is *probably* not the best color.) Whichever way you go, note that absorption devices also absorb stuff in the water, and unfortunately the water might contain an assortment of bacteria. So, remember to remove your tampon soon after exiting the water. This is important. As you know, being a woman takes a little extra effort — but think of the alternative.

# PRE- AND POST-BEACH FASHION

**DO:** Go for comfort and simplicity.

**DON'T:** Match everything (like your towel, rash guard, and back pack).

As far as cover-ups, I like terry cloth long sleeve tops, hooded sweatshirts, and drawstring pants.

I also like microfiber jackets (reversible is cool) and terry shorts. And I love sarongs; they're elegant and sexy.

Want to put it all together? Try a sarong tied low on your hips with a tank top over a printed bikini and a pair of bright colored flip flops. Bring something light with long sleeves if the sun is strong. Oh, and don't forget your fabulous sunnys.

## RETURN OF THE MOLECULE

MENTAL ASPECTS

WHAT TO WEAR

FITNESS

WAVE AND OCEAN KNOWLEDGE

SAFETY AND ETIQUETTE

SURF HISTORY AND HERSTORY

BOARD KNOWLEDGE

HOW TO SURF

You have a nice rolling start on your molecules, and now that you know what to put on, let's see how surfing can improve what you put it on.

# 5. HONE THE TONE:
## BODY SHAPING THE SURFER WAY

### SURFING INTO SHAPE

Surfing will make you stronger all over and improve your endurance. The different movements you perform while surfing will strengthen your tendons and ligaments, and increase muscle tone. Here's how:

### Entering the Ocean

Your fingers, hands, arms, shoulders, and back will all be strengthened as you manage your board on the *inside* (the shore side of the breaking waves) against the rush of the white water. Two months of this and you'll be crushing walnuts in your palm.

### Paddling

While paddling, you're working the back of your neck and the muscles that run along the length of your spine, your lower back, your shoulders, and your lats. Lord help the next boy you hug.

**PADDLING: What Gets Worked**

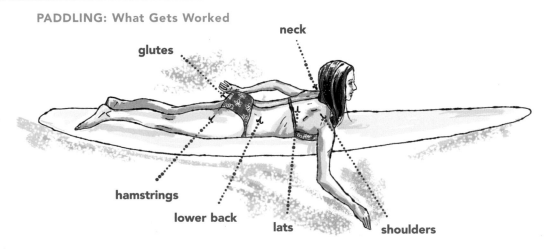

neck

glutes

hamstrings

lower back

lats

shoulders

## Popping Up

Popping up is the quick move that gets you from the prone (flat on your stomach) position to your stance. You'll learn how to pop up in Section 23. Many muscles fire, including all areas of your back, along with your glutes, quads, hamstrings, shoulders, arms, and pecs.

## Wave Riding

Crouching low on your board and twisting to create torque will build strength in your legs and core. Surfing requires that you balance your body on two moving surfaces simultaneously — the board and the water — so you'll have the opportunity to develop exceptional coordination and balance. Yet another reason why surfing rules.

# TRAINING BY SURFING SIMULATION

Here's a newsflash: the best way to improve your surfing is by surfing a lot. If you live away from the coast, though, you can and should improve your potential by simulating surf movements.

## Paddling

Nothing builds paddling strength like paddling. Find a body of water and hop in with your board. I'm thinking a lake here, not a rushing river. Freestyle swimming is your next best bet. It approximates the action of your arms and shoulders when paddling, and will help develop strength. It's not the same, but it's close enough to make a difference.

## Pop–Ups

Do sets of 5 to 20 push-ups. Alternate slow and fast sets so you build both strength and quickness. Try the pop-up and pop-down exercises described in Section 23.

## Balancing

There are various kinds of balancing devices. Indo Board is one. If you're using it indoors, stay clear of sharp corners and glass tables.

Surfers have been known to practice their cross-stepping (Section 30) on a board at a lake in order to develop speed, coordination, and balance.

# GENERAL TRAINING FOR SURFING

## Flexibility

Flexibility is key for surfers; you'll get pulled every which way by the water and wrung like a wet mop. I do yoga four times a week to stay strong and limber.

California strength coach and fitness wizard Franz Snideman gave me five great stretches to increase your flexibility, leave you less prone to injury, and increase your ability to build strength (through better functionality).

Franz says to remember to breathe deeply while stretching.

**Lower Back.** Low Back Rotation Stretch. Surfing requires many rotational movements. Lying on back, bring both knees toward chest; knees pointed straight up. Extend lower leg so there's a 90-degree angle at knee. With arms outstretched at side, rotate legs side to side, with the goal being to touch legs. Do 5–10 reps each side. Keep shoulders on the ground. Don't tense your neck. You need to be moving only out of the lower back.

**Groin.** Seated Groin Stretch. Sit with soles of feet together. Place hands on feet and press knees down to ground (you may use your elbows). You may use elbows to push legs down and to resist on the up move. Do 10 reps.

**Abdominals.** Press Up. It's great as a daily stretch and as a post-surfing stretch. Lie on stomach and put hands in push-up position. Without moving legs, and keeping pelvis on ground, extend torso up, one vertebrae at a time. Keep eyes level and straighten out arms if you can. Hold for two seconds at the top, then lower yourself down. Still breathing deeply? This stretches all of the abdominal wall.

**Hamstrings.** Supine Hami Stretch. Lay on back with legs straight. Wrap towel around one foot, pull toes inward, then pull leg upward. Keep knee straight. Hold for 30 seconds. Repeat with other leg.

**Quadriceps.** Supine Quad Stretch. Sit on heels, put hands behind you and thrust hips upward, shooting belly button straight toward ceiling. Feel it. Go for 30 seconds and both quads get a huge stretch.

## Posture

In athletics, bad posture leads to increased risk of injury. Surfers may tend to develop a hunched posture from the paddling motion. To counteract this — and keep myself upright at least until I'm forty — I seek out exercises that work the shoulder in an opposing fashion. Franz suggests these:

**Reverse Shoulder Wall Press.** Stand with back against wall. Put arms straight out to your sides, with backs of hands against wall. Bend elbows 90 degrees. Press backs of hands hard against wall for 30 seconds. Do 5. Feel it, baby.

**Rowing.** Rowing exercises also help pull the shoulders into better alignment and strengthen the internal rotators. Get two light dumbbells, bend at waist, bend knees slightly, pull with shoulders. At the end of the movement, it's important to squeeze shoulder blades together. Keep stomach tucked and tight. Do 10–15 reps, slow tempo (2 seconds up, 2 seconds down). Keep back arched, chin tucked, and shoulders relaxed.

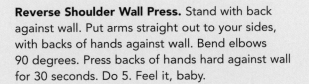

Squeeze it, honey.

## Power

**Twisting.** Learning how to rotate and twist your body with strength, power, and control is essential to success and longevity in surfing. The primary rotational muscles are the internal and external obliques — they're the large muscles that run up from your hips to your rib cage.

**Seated medicine ball twist.** Sit down, bend knees, feet off ground, lean back: touch medicine ball on right side, then left side, and back and forth, first slow, then fast. Do 10 touches on each side. If you don't have a medicine ball, use your little brother.

## Speed

**Sprinting.** Surfing takes a lot of speed — not running speed, of course — speed in the sense of firing off your muscles fast. One way to improve overall speed for *anything*, including surfing, is by sprinting — in the sand, on a track, wherever you like. Make sure to run on the balls of your feet (front third of feet) when sprinting; it will help save your knees. Kickboxing and boxing are also great speed builders.

Okay, troops, we've covered how you should work your muscles; next I'll tell you how to take care of an organ. In fact, the biggest organ humans have.

It's your skin.

# 6. SURVIVAL (OF YOUR SKIN)

I mentioned at the beginning of this book that one of my primary goals is to provide you with memorable safety tips so that your surfing is enjoyable. Well, here's the top tip I could give you: one of the most dangerous things about surfing —

AND **WAY** MORE LIKELY TO CAUSE A **PROBLEM** THAN A **SHARK**.

— is the sun.

Yes, it's true, a little sun is good for you because it helps you produce vitamin D. But it's also true that there's no such thing as a "healthy" tan. A tan is the skin's response to an injury. Sun exposure causes irreversible damage and the damage is cumulative.

THAT MEANS IT **ADDS UP**.

The equation looks like this: Excess sun exposure = tan = sun damage = premature aging and wrinkles, not to mention the long-term possibility of skin cancers, some lethal and some non-lethal. Let's break down this evil system so you know how to beat it.

SCIENCE TIME

## What Does the Skin Do?

It protects you against heat, light, injury, infection, and assists the body in excreting waste. It regulates your body's temperature and it stores water, fat, and the previously mentioned vitamin D. And, without your skin, your other organs would just fall out on the floor and your bones would be visible. That would be a mess.

The skin can perform its duties best if you take care of it. So, I try to avoid things that insult the skin, things like fast-moving objects (cars, other surfers), sharp objects (bagel knives), cigarette smoke, and, of course, the sun.

**WARNING: Ultraviolet Radiation**

## How Does the Sun Insult the Skin?

Primarily by shooting down three types of ultraviolet radiation: UVA, UVB, and UVC. UVCs used to be burned off in the ozone layer (and used by aliens to season their homemade salsa), but with ozone depletion, there's a growing chance of being harmed by these rays, too. UVAs and UVBs are well-understood bad guys: they penetrate into the skin, disrupt skin cell DNA, and cause abnormal growth and mutation. If your immune system doesn't nail these abnormalities, they'll continue to grow and will cause problems, like potentially developing into cancer.

## Here Are Some Facts:

1. Skin cancer is the world's leading form of cancer, by far.
2. A scorching sunburn received as a kid can double your chances of developing skin cancer as an adult.
3. Over 1 million Americans get skin cancer each year.
4. Around 50,000 of those skin cancers will be the lethal form, melanoma.
5. I'm saving the shocking information about Australia, so keep reading.

Hardly anyone gets more sun than a surfer, so I am a fanatic about protecting myself. I don't use a bronzing lotion and I don't go for 4 or 12 or 20. I go for *total* sunblock. I rub waterproof SPF 50 sunblock deep into my face 30 minutes before I go into the sun to give it time to absorb. Yeah, I've heard that anything over SPF 35 doesn't necessarily give added benefit, but I'm not taking any chances. It's a good idea to reapply every 60 to 90 minutes.

## FACE RITUAL

### 30 minutes pre-surfing

1. Apply waterproof sunblock (At least SPF 15. As mentioned, I use SPF 50).

### Before entering the ocean

2. Apply waterproof sunblock stick, opaque (usually only if the sun is intense or it is midday).

### Post-surfing

3. Occasionally use exfoliating face wash, making sure to get off all the sunblock to prevent breakouts.

4. Moisturize.

## HAIR RITUAL

Your hair takes a beating in the ocean from the sun, wind, and salt water. When I had long hair, I used to braid it and tie it up in a bun. Try putting conditioner in your hair before you go in (and before you tie it up). After a session, conditioning is a must.

## BODY RITUAL

Apply sunblock — the highest SPF possible — to all exposed areas. If I'm wearing a wetsuit, I apply it to the tops of my hands and feet, front and back of my neck, and definitely under my chin; the water reflects UV rays onto you.

YOU'VE GOT THE LOOK

45

## SUN PROTECTION
## OUT
## OF THE WATER

Don't think that lounging on or near the beach is the time to get slack. Here's how you should protect yourself when not surfing:

1. **Shade.** Find it as often as possible. Create your own with an umbrella.

2. **Hats.** Go ahead, I'll bet you look super-cute in one.

3. **Clothing:** Long sleeves on tops and full legs bottoms.

4. **Sunglasses:** Invest in a pair with 100% UVA and UVB blocking capability.

Even at age 9 I was sun-conscious.

## Can a Girl Be Cool while Taking Precautions to Avoid the Sun?

Yes. Trashing your skin isn't cool.

## Do Some People Need to Be Extra-Careful?

People with light-colored eyes (green, blue) and light hair are more sun-sensitive. Redheads? Red alert! Where sun-sensitive people have migrated to strong-sun areas, you'll find higher levels of skin cancer. In Australia, where fair-skinned people are exposed to a harsh, ozone layer–deficient environment, two in three residents will be treated for skin cancer in their lifetimes. TWO IN THREE!

P.S. Avoid tanning salon systems that use UVA or UVB. The intensity of rays in certain tanning beds can actually be much higher than those from the sun.

Okay, you get the point. I railed on, but I just want you happy, healthy, and pretty as a picture. Lotion before the ocean, honey.

SINCE YOU SAY THE SUN IS OVERALL MORE OF A THREAT, WE CAN JUST SKIP THE SECTION ON SHARKS, RIGHT?

WE COULD... BUT WE WON'T.

WE'LL GET TO YOU LATER.

Okay, now that you're looking like a surfer, we have a few key pointers on how to act like one.

**PART III**

# THE VIBE OF THE TRIBE

The unwritten code for surfer conduct is — guess what — unwritten. There are some guidelines, though.

# WETIQUETTE

The umbrella concept for surf etiquette is *be respectful* . . . of other surfers while in the water, of people enjoying themselves at the beach, of sea life, of surfers with more expertise than you, and of surfers older than you. Within that umbrella, there is one main rule for surfing:

### THE SURFER TAKING OFF CLOSEST TO THE BREAKING PART OF THE WAVE HAS THE RIGHT OF WAY.

Taking off on a section of the wave *outside of* (here meaning "further along the wave from") another surfer is called *dropping in,* and it's something you should never do. It's rude, dangerous, and leads to collisions. Boys get into fights over this all the time.

An addendum: If you take off outside of the breaking part of the wave, another surfer does not have the right to take off closer to the breaking part of the wave after you're up and riding.

## other Common Sense Rules

### The "You Get to Eat It" Rule

When you're paddling out to the lineup, do not paddle into a wave-rider's path. Give them their wave. This often means you have to paddle behind the surfer, which means you might have to absorb a pounding from the breaking wave.

### The "You Are Responsible for Your Board" Rule

Maintain control of your board and keep it away from others as best you can. Loose boards are dangerous; they're sometimes hard for other surfers to see until it's too late. Boards can injure or even kill, so be careful.

## Localism

Localism is the term applied to a group of surfers being protective of their surf spot — they simply don't want to share the waves. Locals can be hostile to newcomers, so I recommend that beginners avoid localized spots. That said, you should know the basic rules for working your way into a spot when you're a competent surfer.

- Don't make a scene. It's best not to show up with a pack of friends.

- Let the locals have their choice of waves at first.

- Don't paddle out into the middle of a lineup. Start on the outside and wait your turn.

## Wetiquette Sum-Up

It's really not difficult to be considerate. If you can't, try another sport, like hockey.

## KOOK-A-RAMA

We all do kook things occasionally, and we did even more of them when we were beginners. That's no excuse, though. What follows is a list of twenty things kooks do. Avoid them.

### Pre-Surfing Don'ts

1. Drop your board when taking it off the roof rack.

2. Instead of dropping your board when removing it from the roof rack, place it down with a *thump*. Meet your new ding.

3. Rest your board behind someone else's parked car. Presume that car will stay parked.

4. Leave your car key perched on the back left tire so anyone can borrow your vehicle while you are in the water.

5. Put your wetsuit on zipped up in the front.

6. Sit and/or stand on your board on dry land.

7. As you begin your walk to the beach from the parking lot, bang your board into your own car's bumper.

8. Then bang your board into other things as you walk: surfers, skaters, cyclists, other cars. Carve as large a swath as possible.

9. Carry your board with the deck against your body so the wax smudges onto your wetsuit and you have to hire a nuclear waste cleanup team to remove it.

10. After applying wax, take the unused portion of the wax bar and hurl it into the ocean, seeing how far you can make it skip.

### Surfing Don'ts

11. Surf in spots where the waves are above your level of expertise with surfers who are above your level of expertise. Snap back at anyone who wonders aloud what you're doing there.

12. Never look left or right while preparing to take off. If you see someone taking off behind you, just start your ride anyway.

13. Paddle out into the path of wave-riding surfers so you minimize your contact with white water.

### On the Beach Don'ts

14. Leave your board deck-up on the sand (Wax melts, remember?)

15. Walk around everywhere with your leash strapped on.

16. Leave candy wrappers and cola cans on the beach for someone else to clean up.

## Post-Surfing Don'ts

17. Drop your board while rinsing it off.

18. Never thoroughly rinse your wetsuit off, allowing all manner of biological material to replicate and then merge with your skin the next time you suit up.

19. Secure your board fins-down on the roof rack.

20. Wear your wetsuit in the car. Wear it into shops and restaurants, too.

# ENTRANCES AND EXITS

The sooner you show up to the beach looking and acting like a surfer, the better. Here's a start:

## Arriving

◎ Remove and load your board with care.

◎ Upon arrival, add a layer of wax to the deck of your board. It feels good to have some fresh, sticky stuff under your feet.

◎ If you are a raw beginner, ask an expert about the conditions. The bunny fru-fru girl sprawled out on a pink towel charbroiling herself is probably not the right person. Try a lifeguard.

◎ Proper board carrying is an under-rated skill. The basic technique is to carry your honey under one arm, deck out, fins back, with the nose pointed slightly down.

If your board is too wide for you to get your arm around it, you have options:

**Board on Head.** Fold up your beach towel and place it on your head. Place your board on top of the towel. Make sure the deck of your board is up — unless you want wax in your hair for dramatic styling opportunities.

**Crook of Elbow.** The board rests in the crook of your elbow and on your forearm. It leans against your shoulder. Your hand cups the rail from underneath. Your other arm swings casually at your side as you absorb the impressed looks of other surfers.

## Dealing with Your Gear

At a minimum, you should bring water, sunblock, a hat, and a first-aid kit (see Section 16) to the beach.

Car keys are an issue; some surfers hide them on their cars and that's fine if a) no one is watching you while you do it; and b) no one goes looking for it. Two bad assumptions. Cars are stolen from surf spots all the time. Once when I surfed County Line (north of Malibu), a guy came back to his parking space with his son and his new Mercedes was gone. He had hidden the key near the gas cap, which seems like one of the first places someone would look.

One alternative is stringing your key through a shoelace and wearing it around your neck (under your wetsuit). Another is burying it at the bottom of your gear bag and taking the bag to the sand. If you go that route, take a brightly colored towel so you can monitor your stuff from the water. Try to find someone trustworthy to keep an eye on your bag. This is preferable to leaving it completely unguarded.

Nothing is 100 percent safe. If you do leave your key, scan for sketchy people. Stuff gets stolen from beaches all the time; it's another risk of the sport, but then, as you've become a surfer and have connected so profoundly with nature, material things aren't that important anymore, now, are they?

And last but not least . . .

# 8. TALK THE TALK
## SURF LINGO

When it comes to talking like a surfer, I suggest you be yourself and not force it. There is, however, a sizeable surfing vocabulary, most of which can be substituted by just saying "dude" every other word. Use it as an exclamation or an imperative. Use it to describe or call out to a man, woman, boy, girl, or animal. By adding an inflection, raise of the eyebrow, or head nod, "dude" can mean:

**Hello**
**Absolutely!**
**Over there**
**Check out that guy/girl**

"Dude" can also be used to ask questions, like:

**What's wrong?**
**What is this we're eating?**
**Why is your face bleeding?**

DUDE!

Yeah, I'm kidding. I actually dislike that word a lot, and when it slips out of me from time to time, I pray no one notices. If you'd like a head start on surf lingo, read my glossary in Appenchix A. It's organized by categories, making the info easier to peruse and retain. Practice the words, form sentences with them, and, yes, feel free to make flash cards.

Soon it will feel natural for you to say things like,

NICOLE GOT TUBED AND SPIT, AND RIGHT BEFORE SHE KICKED OUT, SOME SPONGER DROPPED IN ON HER AND SHE JUST MISSED RAKING HIM. HE WIPED OUT, GOT PITCHED, AND THEN WENT OVER THE FALLS. GOT NUKED. IT WAS GNARLY. WE LAUGHED, THOUGH, IT WAS SO RIGHT. CAN YOU PASS THE GUACAMOLE?

to your friends. All without using the word "dude" once! Smile accordingly, because I think a lot of this lingo is pretty corny.

Here's a visual preview of some essential surfing lingo, which focuses on the anatomy of a wave.

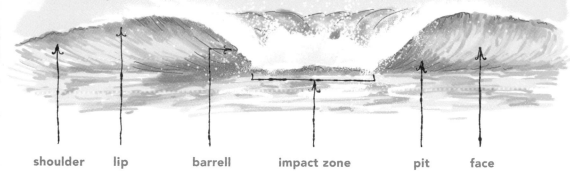

shoulder    lip    barrell    impact zone    pit    face

## Estimating Wave Height

Wave height is one of the most common things brought up in a conversation among surfers. There are two ways to measure wave height: the Hawaiian way and the way of everywhere else.

In Hawaii, waves are measured by the size of the back of the wave. It doesn't make a lot of sense — no one rides the back of the wave, now do they? — it's just tradition. There's a macho component, too, since the heights are played way down: Waves are usually estimated at a little less than one-half the height of the face of the wave. Here's a formula (presented just for fun) for calculating Hawaiian wave heights:

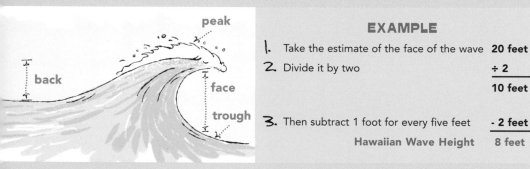

### EXAMPLE

| | | |
|---|---|---|
| 1. | Take the estimate of the face of the wave | **20 feet** |
| 2. | Divide it by two | **÷ 2** |
| | | **10 feet** |
| 3. | Then subtract 1 foot for every five feet | **- 2 feet** |
| | **Hawaiian Wave Height** | **8 feet** |

A 20-foot bomb becomes an 8-footer. It almost sounds surfable, huh?

The rest of the world estimates wave height by the face of the wave from trough to peak. Waves might be referred to in terms of feet, but they're best expressed in relation to your height, as in: ankle biter, knee-high, waist-high, chest-high, shoulder-high, head-high, overhead, double overhead, etc. As a beginner, it's important to start small, being sure to stay less than waist high. You can still have ten tons of fun on waves this size.

# 9. WAVE GURU

A good surfer knows the dynamics of waves and the ocean, and a large part of this knowledge comes from experience in the water. In Section 20, I'll provide some pointers on how to begin experiencing the water. There's an intellectual component you should know, too: it's basic waterwoman knowledge, and it will provide you with more words to supplement your growing surfing vocabulary.

## Where Waves Come From

Waves typically are generated by the wind, which is often generated by storms out at sea. The wind blowing against the water creates a ripple, and the ripple provides a good surface for the wind to push against, thus stretching out the ripple.

The ripples that get enough energy to move on their own without the wind become swells. Swells most often travel in sets of around three to twelve. (Note: sometimes "swell" and "wave" are used interchangeably.) After a wave gets enough energy to move on its own without the wind, it can travel thousands of miles and end up at a beach near you. Trippy, but true.

Waves break when they've grown too steep. Whitecaps form and the wave curls over when it reaches a water depth that is about 1.33 times its height. The sand floor might cause the wave-break ratio to become critical, or it might result from the wave hitting a reef, which happens abruptly and causes big waves with a lot of force.

SCIENCE TIME

Local winds at a beach blowing *onshore* (toward the shore) usually make for sloppy and choppy waves, known as *wind slop*). The word surfers love to hear is *offshore*, because offshore winds often make the waves stand up deliciously for our long-riding enjoyment.

## Ride the Tide

Let me take you back to sixth grade (Okay, fourth for some and ninth or tenth for others) for a little quiz on the basic information you should know about tides. Your score will go down on your permanent record. Ready? Begin.

The ebb and flow of tides is caused by the _____ forces of the _____ and the _____ playing on the _____. Approximately every _____ hours the tide changes out, going from _____ to _____ or _____ to _____.

Pencils down.

**Answers:** gravitational, sun, moon, Earth, six, high, low, low, high.

Knowing the tide changes is important to surfers. Typically, a surf spot is best under a specific tide condition. For example, some spots work best at high tide, some at low, and some a couple of hours before high tide. Here are three huge generalities:

◎ If the waves are slow and mushy, a lower tide might speed it up and add shape.

◎ If the waves are *closing out* (a closeout wave is one that breaks across its face, all at once), a higher tide might slow it down and make it ridable.

◎ An incoming tide can often add extra push to a swell (that is, increase the size and power of the waves).

To maximize your chances of getting good waves, your best bet is to ask a local surfer or surf shop what tide condition is best for the spot you're interested in. They'll also have tide tables so you can plan your week (or year) accordingly.

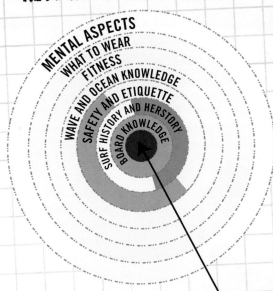

# RETURN OF THE MOLECULE

MENTAL ASPECTS
WHAT TO WEAR
FITNESS
WAVE AND OCEAN KNOWLEDGE
SAFETY AND ETIQUETTE
SURF HISTORY AND HERSTORY
BOARD KNOWLEDGE

HOW TO SURF

**Look at this:** your safety gene has been activated through skin care, and you're getting the lingo, etiquette, and are making progress on your wave and ocean knowledge. Molecule conversion, underway.

# 10. LICKS AND FLICKS

We can't surf all the time, right? Luckily, they've created things to fill our down time: music and movies that remind us of surfing. You might enjoy this part of surf culture — anything that combines surfing and art can get you feeling the vibe and bring you closer to the sport. You also get to bask in the language and, in the case of videos and film, you might even learn something that builds your skills (and provides more uses of the word "dude").

## LICKS

I like to listen to all kinds of music and I can't say that just one type puts me in the mood for surfing. There doesn't seem to be any surf-specific music anymore. During the sixties though, there was. If you'd like to explore this part of surfing history, check out groups like the Ventures, the Chantays, the Surfaris, and Dick Dale — the King of the Surf Guitar. Somehow, they manage to capture in sound what a surfer on a wave looks like.

Did you see *Pulp Fiction?* The song with the wild guitar played over the opening credits is called "Miserlou" — it's a Dale song — and if anything on the planet sounds like a surfer ripping up a wave, that does. Songs like "Pipeline" and "Wipeout" achieve a similar effect.

The Beach Boys' music is timeless and beautiful. Their albums *Pet Sounds* and *Endless Summer* are filled with great songs: "God Only Knows," "Good Vibrations," and let's not forget "Surfer Girl." They helped define for the rest of America and the world what the beach and summer was about. Wanna know something? Only one Beach Boy was a surfer (Dennis Wilson), which is pretty good evidence that you don't have to actually surf to make yourself at home with the surfer's vibe.

## FLICKS

### Home Release

There are a gazillion DVDs and videos of surfers doing their thing on practically every surfable spot on Earth. Pick your favorite surfer and chances are that there's some footage to watch. My favorite video producers are Taylor Steele and Bill Ballard. Bill, in fact, shot a video of top women pro surfers called *Blue Crush* before the theatrical film was made.

I'll also watch anything featuring my friends Lisa Anderson, Rochelle Ballard, Keala Kennelly, and Andy and Bruce Irons. Okay, I'm biased, I love them. I grew up with all of them (except Lisa) on Kauai, and I find what they do to be amazing. Check them out for yourself. Lay back and let the action roll around in your head. If you want to get better at surfing, watch the best.

### Theatrical Release

It's always good fun (or *insulting*, depending on how you look at it) to watch how fast characters in movies learn to surf. In *Point Break*, Keanu Reeves (as Johnny Utah) not only learns too fast, he utters a major surf-dissing line when he says surfing is something for "little rubber people who don't shave yet." *Nice.*

In *North Shore*, Matt Adler as Rick Kane spends one summer in Hawaii and he's ready for the big contest at Pipeline. *Go get 'em, amigo!*

Surf fiction is also a good place to find standard surfer stereotypes: There's blond and dumb (Sam Bottoms in *Apocalypse Now*), blond and high (Sean Penn in *Fast Times at Ridgemont High*), and blond and mystical (Patrick Swayze in *Point Break*, and me in real life — ha ha.)

Among the fictional surf films, *Big Wednesday* has some of the most convincing characters. It's a realistic portrait of what it was like to grow up as a surfer in Malibu in the sixties, as the screenwriter/director John Milius actually did. Milius was also the co-writer of *Apocalypse Now*, which I included in my rating grid for surf movies because it has a long surfing sequence in which Robert Duval cranks out a ton of great lines.

## Bars-of-Wax Rating System

From **0** (*Coulda Been Better*) to **5** (*Epic*)

|  | BODS | SURF ACTION | SURFING UNDER GUNFIRE |
|---|---|---|---|

**1959** **GIDGET**

Coming-of-age story of a teen girl at Malibu beach. The novel helped launch surf culture in America, and the movie provided another push. Sweet film, worth seeing, but you might be shocked to see teens depicted so innocently.

**1966** **THE ENDLESS SUMMER**

Bruce Brown's masterpiece about two guys searching the globe for the perfect wave. Great for anyone and a must-see for surfers. The movie captures the spirit of our sport.

**1978** **BIG WEDNESDAY**

Three Malibu friends find out there's more to surfing than life. Excellent film. Peter Townend and Ian Cairns stunt-surf, and we get to see wave-carving artist Gerry Lopez doing his thing.

**1979** **APOCALYPSE NOW**

Extended sequence with Robert Duval as the insane Colonel Kilgore. He uses attack helicopters to secure a beach so his personal surf team can shred . . . while being shot at. He gives his men a choice: surf or fight. Which would you do?

**1987** **NORTH SHORE**

Arizona wave pool surf champ (chuckle) goes Hawaii to surf the big waves (chuckle). Gets himself a lesson in the ways of surfing. Tons of pro surfers have cameo roles. The film has cult status among some surfers, and there are plenty that can and will quote from it. Decide for yourself if that's a good thing.

| | | BODS | SURF ACTION | SURFING UNDER GUNFIRE | |
|---|---|---|---|---|---|
| 1991 | **POINT BREAK** |  | | | Keanu Reeves has to infiltrate a gang of surfers who might be robbing banks, so he needs to learn how to surf real fast. At least it's a cute chick surfer who teaches him. |
| 1994 | **THE ENDLESS SUMMER II** |  | | | Follow up to the original, almost thirty years later. Two new guys, lots more global surfing. Hamilton and Lopez appear also. |
| 2002 | **BLUE CRUSH** | ★ | ★ | | Chix teach dix new trix. |
| 2003 | **STEP INTO LIQUID** |  | | | This time a Brown (Bruce's son Bryan) films women. Keala Kennelly, Rochelle Ballard, and Layne Beachley join Laird Hamilton, his foil board, and others, on a big wave hunt. Incredible footage of monster waves being towed-in on. |

★ You rate it.

If you just feel like seeing sand and water on the screen, here's a list of beach movies. They go from the silly (*Beach Blanket Bingo*) to the serious (*Lifeguard*), and some have a little surfing in them.

**1961** *Gidget Goes Hawaiian, Blue Hawaii*
**1963** *Beach Party*
**1964** *Surf Party, Muscle Beach Party, The Horror of Party Beach, For Those Who Think Young, Bikini Beach, Ride the Wild Surf*
**1965** *A Swingin' Summer, Beach Blanket Bingo, The Girls on the Beach, One Way Wahine, How to Stuff a Wild Bikini, Wild on the Beach, The Beach Girls and the Monster, Beach Ball*
**1966** *Wild Wild Winter, The Ghost in the Invisible Bikini, Out of Sight*
**1967** *It's A Bikini World, Catalina Caper, Don't Make Waves.*
**1968** *The Sweet Ride*

**1974** *Malibu Hot Summer* (re-released in '87 as *Sizzle Beach USA*)
**1976** *Lifeguard*
**1977** *Summer City*
**1978** *Malibu Beach*
**1979** *California Dreamin'*
**1984** *Surf 2*
**1987** *Back to the Beach,* **Surf Nazis Must Die**\*\*
**1988** *Aloha Summer*
**1989** *Under the Boardwalk*
**1990** *An American Summer*
**1995** *Blue Juice*
**2000** *Psycho Beach Party*

\*\* LAKE AWARD FOR THE BEST SURF-RELATED TITLE OF A FILM.

# 11. BEHIND THE SCENES OF BLUE CRUSH

**BLUE CRUSH**

IF YOU WANT TO FEEL THE RUSH
YOU HAVE TO TAKE THE RISK

Since we're talking surf films, let's talk about one near to my heart, and one that is pretty focused when it comes to the subject of girls and surfing.

Surprisingly, working on the film allowed for the least amount of surfing I can ever remember doing. There's a lot of downtime on movie sets, so I'd be sitting around on the beach watching perfect wave after perfect wave roll by. The actors were only allowed to surf when the surfing scenes were being filmed. The reason was a combination of insurance-liability issues and the fact that they didn't want to have to redo our hair. Of course, I felt privileged and happy to be there, but watching those waves was heartbreaking.

You'll know you've graduated to being a surfer when you see waves and actually feel physical pain because you can't ride them.

Four girls, one board, big problem

Director John Stockwell, protecting us from the advancing tide

I bounced pretty hard off the reef today. It's the biggest day since I've been here. I'm thankful to have seen Cloudbreak like this. I had to go sit on the boat until the bleeding stopped so I wouldn't attract sharks. My chest & right arm got grated, the reef here is sharp... beautiful though.

# PART IV

# SEA HAZARDS

# 12. SURF GIRLS ARE NOT EASY

One big surfing hazard is sun, and another biggie is your own board (which we'll discuss in Sections 16 and 24). That leaves sea creatures. Let's start with the human variety.

## How to Deal with Guys Hitting On You IN the Water

Yes, surf girls are by definition cute and surfer boys might be smitten. Depending on the frequency of the sets and the size of the waves, there might be time to kill out there. Boys have ideas about how to fill that time.

If a boy hits on you and you're interested, well, game on. If you're not interested, here are a few suggestions:

1. Field his highly original questions curtly. Do not ask him any of your own. Stare intensely at the horizon and the hopefully-soon-to-be-arriving set.

2. After flawlessly riding a wave in, paddle out to a different section.

3. Some boys need something less subtle. Tell him you'd consider meeting him later, right after you return from your appointment with your (select one) psychiatrist/infectious disease specialist/sex-change counselor.

On the other hand, the attention can be flattering; it just depends. The one thing I do suggest if you end up with a surfer boyfriend is not to get between him and his surfing . . . just like you wouldn't want him to get between you and yours. Give him breathing room and don't take offense if he wants to surf occasionally without you, especially if he's more advanced. He will greatly appreciate the space.

## How to Deal with Guys Hitting On You OUT of the Water

Of course, the trouble doesn't just happen in the water. Here is a real incident that happened to me near a Southern California beach.

I wish I was the only girl who ever had this conversation, but I seriously doubt that's true. The best way to deal with beach-side situations like this is hit the "ignore" button. If you can't deal, remove yourself from the vicinity. Remind yourself that heavenly surfing is only a few minutes away — that'll take the sting out of almost anything.

# 13. THE SHARK SECTION

Now that we've covered boys, let's move
on to less dangerous sea creatures.

EVERYONE IS AFRAID OF SHARKS! OKAY, WE GET IT!!
THEY CAN BE AS BIG AS AN S.U.V. AND ARE RELENTLESS,
MERCILESS, KILLING MACHINES!!

BACK TO THAT AGAIN?

BUT KEEP IN MIND THAT THE ODDS ARE *WITH YOU*—IT'S UNLIKELY THAT YOU'LL EVER EVEN **SEE** A SIZEABLE SHARK!

BETTER.

**SCIENCE TIME**

The U.S. Shark Attack File lightning statistic looks like this:

◉ People killed by lightning in U.S. coastal states from 1959 to 1994 (their most recent data): **1,618**

◉ People killed by sharks in waters off of those states during that same time period: **only 17**

Although the chances are remote, the reality is, as a surfer, you're in their territory and there is a risk. So let's take a peek at this fearsome predator.

There are over 350 species of shark but just 3 main types that attack people: great white, bull, and tiger. Sharks are generally unpredictable, but there are some ways to reduce the chances of an encounter.

## Reducing Your Chances of Encountering Sharks

1. Don't surf at dusk or dawn; that's when sharks are most often feeding.

2. Don't surf where there are a lot of seals, sea lions, or sea turtles, or areas where they breed.

3. Avoid river mouths, since sharks like to feed and rest there (at river mouths, the water might be rushing fast enough to allow sharks to stay stationary and still draw oxygen).

4. Avoid areas between sand bars and steep dropoffs.

5. Surf in groups. Sharks often go for individual targets.

6. Don't wear shiny objects like jewelry. Sharks might mistake them for fish scales.

7. Sharks do have a highly acute sense of smell, and they do go for blood, so if you're nervous about sharks, you might stay out of the water if you have any bloody cuts or are menstruating.

## Shark Attack

Never jump off your surfboard and attack a shark; it's show-offy.

If you get attacked, there are no exact rules on what to do. It's rare for the victim to see it coming. If you end up in the clutches of its jaws, you might gouge it in the eye or punch it in the snout. It's worth a shot. Hopefully, the shark will realize it has mistaken you for its normal food and will sulk away after a quick hit.

Most people who die from shark attacks die from loss of blood, not from being consumed. Stop any bleeding as soon as possible with direct pressure. If you're alone, you have a real problem. If there's someone else you're out with and they are the bite-ee, you may not even have time to get the person to shore — that could take ten minutes — so you might have to take action on the water.

If a limb has been munched on, put direct pressure on the wound to slow or stop the bleeding and proceed to safety. In a rare case of complete amputation, Holt Blanchard and his son, Byron, used a rash guard as a tourniquet to tie off the shoulder of Kauaiian Bethany Hamilton (the teenage surf princess who lost her arm to a shark in 2003). Without that, she probably would not have survived. By the time she got to the hospital, half of her blood was gone.

You have literally minutes or seconds to stop a bad bleeder before it's too late, so whatever you do, do it fast, and get out of the water before the shark and/or his buddies come back for more.

# 14. STINGS, BITES, AND POISON

**WATCH YOUR STEP**

Depending on what part of the globe you are in, there are a host of other creatures that could cause problems for you.

**Jellyfish** give a painful sting — their tentacles inject a poison and keep pumping it in as long as they're attached. If you get stung, wash off the tentacles and stingers with rubbing alcohol. Jellyfish cause an allergic reaction, so antihistamines may help. It's very rare, but if you happen to get covered and stung over a massive area, it could be life-threatening. Even the dismembered tentacles of jellyfish may be active, so avoid them, too.

**Stingrays** sit on the ocean floor, typically in warm, sandy, shallow waters. They're passive; you're likely to have a problem with them only if you step directly on them. If you do, you'll wish you hadn't — when they strike, they drive their poisonous stinger into you like a hammered nail. Excruciating pain follows.

**Stingray Hit Treatment:** Remove debris from the wound with a sterile pad or have a doctor do it. Disinfect using something like Betadyne (see Section 16 for details). The ray's toxin is heat-sensitive, so the best way to ease the pain and speed recovery is to soak the affected area in water as hot as you can stand (without burning your skin) for about 90 minutes. Follow up with a doctor.

## How to Avoid Getting Hit By a Stingray

1. Scan downward as you walk in the shallows to avoid stepping directly on one.
2. Shuffle your feet forward instead of clomping down. This action will scare up Mr. Ray and usually send him on his way.
3. Be on your board as much as possible. This makes your Surfer Molecules happy, also.

## Other Sea Creatures

**Sea urchins** live in the hollows of reefs and can send their spines into you if you step on them, providing a painful sting. **Eels** dwell in small caves and tunnels and might bite you if they are disturbed and feel threatened. **Barracudas** have been known to nibble on people, too.

In the South Pacific and Indian Ocean, there are **sea snakes** that have lethal venom. That region also has **stone-fish**, a member of the scorpionfish family, which are the most venomous fish in the sea. It pumps poison through spines that run along its back, and if it gets you, you could easily die. The stonefish can be found at depths of 130 feet, or sitting in the exposed sand of tidal inlets.

## Live Another Day Story

I was standing on a dock in Tahiti a few years ago and saw this weird rock next to a piling. I thought about kicking it, but instead I poked it with a stick. The rock swam away; whether it was a deadly member of the scorpionfish family or just one that can hurt you real bad, I'm not sure, but the lessons remain the same: always be extra careful when messing around in or near the water. Ask the lifeguard or knowledgeable locals what to look out for, be careful where you step, and minimize your impulse to pet the animals. If you do get bitten, stung, or injected with poison, see a doctor as soon as you can.

**Legal Liability Transferred Completely to Reader**

# 15. BACTERIA AND THE SOLUTIONS TO POLLUTION

Storm drain runoff, sewage release, and dumping are enemies of the surfer. Like the sun, ocean pollution is a hazard that will be encountered by 100 percent of surfers. Step into the ocean and you'll encounter everything from plastic bags to cigarette butts to bacteria from human waste. In polluted seas, ear and skin infections are common and hepatitis A has been known to be contracted.

Because a lot of pollution in city areas is carried into the ocean by storm drains, one way to minimize your exposure is to stay out of the ocean for two to three days after it rains. Another way is to help solve the problem and contribute to keeping the oceans clean. Frankly, it's the duty of all surfers. If you're interested in helping, here are five things you can do:

1. **Don't dump anything into storm drains; they're for rainwater only.** Garbage should go into cans and old motor oil should be trapped and taken to a gas station. Doing some gardening or lawn maintenance? Use less herbicides and chemicals; they get washed into storm drains, too. Instead, use compost or fertilizer. Scoop up pet waste. Don't throw cigarette butts on the ground. Pick up litter.

2. **Encourage your local city council to maintain funds for city sewage line repair and replacement.** When these lines get old and crack, raw sewage can pour into the ocean. Get them to upgrade sewage treatment plants while you're at it. When cities start spending public money on sports stadiums, ask how the funds for infrastructure are doing.

3. **Minimize harsh chemicals and materials going down your household drains.** Use phosphate-free laundry detergent. Use baking soda or "green" cleaning products instead of products with hazardous chemicals. Do not flush non-biodegrable products down the toilet.

4. **Help protect ocean wildlife.** Are you a fisherwoman? Don't dispose of fishing lines or nets in the water; fish get tangled up in them. Cut open plastic 6-pack rings. Party girl? Don't release helium balloons outside; they can float to the ocean, where birds and fish can choke on them.

5. **Get involved.** Report illegal dumping to the EPA or the Coast Guard. Appenchix C has a list of environmental organizations dedicated to keeping the oceans clean. Some are taking the lead in working with local governments to keep ocean health as a priority, and they need our support to accomplish this.

## Bacteria and Reef Cuts

Bacteria can also get you in another way. Razor-sharp coral reef populates many oceans and can open up nasty, irregular cuts. Often debris will lodge in the wound and it must be removed completely to help prevent infection. It's usually too painful to do yourself, so after you use a disinfectant, go to a doctor. Untreated wounds can lead to slow healing, scars, and infections. Pus in the wound and red streaks on your skin spreading from the wound are two signs of infection. Untreated infections can lead to serious to systemic conditions, so don't be lazy.

If you must get to a surf spot separated by shallow reef, try flipping your board over, fins up, and paddling over it. Be mindful of the fins and the fact that that the board will be slippery on the non-waxed side.

There's a good chance you'll get banged up occasionally while surfing. While reef and scattered rocks might get you, it's your board that's going to seem like it's magnetically attracted to you. While beginners are a particular hazard to themselves because of inexperience and forgetfulness, surfers at any level are at risk for injury. Let's start with the psychological aspects. How do you deal with it if you end up with some unsightly scrapes, bruises, or cuts? Get over it, that's how.

As far as the physical effects, I asked Greg Mattson, MD (a forty-year surfer), and Michael Lauer, MD, of the La Jolla Medical Clinic what you should do. Some of their wisdom is shared here. Always consult a doctor if you get injured.

**Legal Liability Transferred
Completely to Reader**

## First—Aid Kit

Carry one in your car or with you when you're traveling. The basic components are Betadyne (a disinfectant), rubbing alcohol, sterile bandages, an ACE bandage, and athletic tape. Quick Ice may come in handy also. Betadyne also comes impregnated in a sterile brush; find that baby if you can.

## Injury Treatment

**Scrapes.** Scrub with Betadyne, rinse, apply triple antibiotic such as Neosporin, then bandage to keep clean and avoid sun exposure, which causes scars.

**Bruises.** Broken capillaries bleeding into the skin can cause a rainbow of discoloration: green, yellow, blue, red, and black, for starters. If you can get ice on it within thirty minutes of the incident, you can reduce the swelling and severity. Concealing makeups and products like Dermablend are available to cover a bruise, or you can shine a flashlight on it, flex repeatedly, and pretend it's a lava lamp.

**Lacerations.** A deep cut, through the skin layers to the fat, likely needs to be stitched close. Before you get to a doctor, you can go through the scrape-disinfecting procedure. The fastest way to heal a deep laceration with minimal scarring is to have it cleaned thoroughly and sutured on the same day as the injury. Delaying this treatment will only result in longer healing with subsequent infections. This equates to longer downtime from surfing. Depending on the location of the wound, healing may occur within five to ten days if treated properly. An infected wound may take months to heal, so be smart!

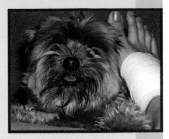

Cute, furry animals help ease any discomfort.

**Sprained Ankle.** If you jump off your board in the shallows, you're asking for trouble. RICE is the standard treatment: Rest, Ice, Compression (ACE bandage), and Elevation (above the level of your heart). Ice is usually effective for the first 72 hours, and the sooner applied after the incident, the better.

**Sore Muscles and Ribs.** Just like any workout, you will get sore (back, neck, shoulders, arms, etc.). Take a day off from surfing and work out other muscle groups by running or bike riding. You'll be amazed what twenty-four hours of rest will do for a muscle group. Prevention: Work harder on your out-of-the water training. Review Section 5 for a jumpstart.

While you're in the water, if you feel fatigued but are too lazy to paddle in to rest, try stretching. Get off your board and curl yourself in a ball. This will stretch the muscles in an opposing fashion to your paddling position. Rotate your neck, too.

**Rubbing Rashes.** Parts of you that press against your board, like your inner thighs (while you're sitting) or chest, may get a rash. It should eventually go away. Try moisturizing lotion. Of course, if you're not sure whether it's just a rubbing rash, check with your doctor.

**Sunburn.** An anti-inflammatory medication (aspirin or ibuprofen) will give relief as well as Vitamin E spray and aloe vera. Ask your doctor. Moisturize to help with peeling.

## Scar Prevention

Keep wounds moist until they heal. Excess scab from scrapes can be soaked off. Aloe has been shown to have some healing and anti-scarring properties, but it should be applied only when the wound is dry and sealed. Aloe (raw or otherwise) is not sterile and if placed in an open wound can cause infection.

## Back into the ocean?

Saltwater can be therapeutic for muscle aches, pains, and swelling. If the ocean is dirty, however, any open wound is subject to infection. So, it's best to stay out of the water until even minor wounds are healed.

Rell Sun

PART V

# THE HERSTORY OF SURFING

# 17. MODERN CHIX PICKUP STIX

When we left off our blockbuster story of the origin of surfing, we were in the early twentieth century, and surfing was starting to take off again in Hawaii and for the first time in California. So, how did we women get here from there? Via the pioneering spirit of over seventy years of women surfers and a lot of butt-kicking action in the water, that's how. Here's a look at some of the contributors.

## 1930s-1950s:
### THE ORIGINAL HONEYS

In California, surfer and sometime-starlet Mary Ann Hawkins started infil-trating the line-up in Orange County and Malibu during the thirties and forties. She surfed well and looked real good doing it. That inspired a core group of young Malibu honeys who, in the early 1950s, advanced the sport for women with the help of a technical innovation — the Girl Board, which was way lighter than boards of the day and made surfing more user-friendly for smaller people (like girls). The Girl Board was invented by three men, which proved once again that men are good for something.

Mary Ann Hawkins

The Calhouns at Makaha: Robin, Marge, and Candy

One of the Malibu girls taught a woman named Marge Calhoun to surf, and a few years later, in 1958, Calhoun became the first mainlander to win the world's biggest surf competition at the time, the Makaha Invitational in Hawaii. Oh yeah, and let's not forget that when she won she was well into her thirties and had two teenage daughters. Not bad, Mom.

Around the same time, the novel *Gidget* and its movie follow-up were released. Such media offerings connecting girls with surfing put a lot more girls in the water.

Gidget

Linda Benson

# 1960s:
## QUANTUM LEAP

Calhoun inspired a legion of surfers and surf champions, including Linda Benson, who won at Makaha in 1959 at the age of 15 (and repeated in 1960), and Joyce Hoffman, an athletic surfer who bumped up the profile of women's surfing when she became one of the first women surfers to attract substantial sponsorships.

And then came Margo.

The late sixties brought a radical new presence in the form of Margo Godfrey Oberg, a La Jolla shredder

Joyce Hoffman

who, in 1968, won her first world championship at the age of 15. Margo surfed hyper-aggressively, with a take-no-prisoners attitude about contests. Many who saw her say she was the Michael Jordan of women's surfing — they say she changed the reference point for all women surfers to follow. She was one of the first women to connect maneuvers and work a wave with the athleticism of a guy. She was also one of one of the first accomplished female big-wave riders. Oberg retired from surfing in the early seventies to start a family, but then came back to win world titles in '77, '79, '80, and '82. Mom power, again!

Margo Oberg

*Margo Oberg*
WORLD SURFING CHAMPION

CAR COURTESY OF
SHELLY MOTO
ALA MOANA BLVD & NIN

# THE 1970s–1980s:
## TIME TO ORGANIZE

The seventies were notable for the beginning of the women's professional movement. During the early seventies, prize money was minimal for women and there was no organized tour. Most women pros worked regular jobs to support themselves, and it was not unusual to for them to sell possessions — like their cars, as La Jollan Debbie Beacham did — to get money to travel to events.

The seeds of change were planted in 1975, when savvy pro surfer Jericho Poppler founded the Women's International Surfing Association, the first organization dedicated to promoting women's surfing. She didn't stop there. In 1979, Poppler founded the WPS (Women's Professional Surfers), which was meant to be a union of sorts to help women increase prize money and their general status.

Things started improving, though slowly. Then Beacham picked up the reins of the WPS in '81 and organized the first women's professional tour. She attracted major sponsors, and then spearheaded and negotiated the merger with the men's tour, the APS. Beacham then won the '82 world title. Nice year for Debbie, I'd say.

Sponsorship built slowly during the eighties.

Margo Oberg

The late, great Rell Sunn,
Queen of Makaha ('60s-'80s)

Freida Zamba

The new tour was dominated by Freida Zamba and Wendy Botha, who each won four world titles between '83 and '92.

# THE 1990s AND 2000s:
## THE FUTURE IS NOW

In the nineties, Lisa Anderson became the first woman surfer to cross over into general celebrity status. What inspires me about Lisa's surfing is her combination of grace and power; what inspires me about *Lisa* is her will and perseverance. Her story is a great one: she left Florida when she was 16, bound for California, after writing her parents a note saying that she would become a world surfing champion. She kicked around Huntington Beach for eight years, and then it happened. In '94, she won her first world title, followed it up with three more in a row, and is now considered one of the greatest female surfers ever.

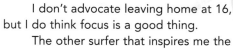
Lisa Anderson and Me

I don't advocate leaving home at 16, but I do think focus is a good thing.

The other surfer that inspires me the most is Keala Kennelly. When we were kids, she set an example for me that being a girl doesn't have to limit you. She surfed big waves, just as big as the guys — and we're talking some serious waves.

Keala certainly has taken the phrase "Go big or go home" to heart: she ranks among the world's top women surfers and is a fearless big-wave and barrel rider.

Keala Kennelly

Layne Beachley

And finally, Layne Beachley: she's rewritten the record books for women's surfing, winning six consecutive world titles. Her accomplishments, along with her big-wave riding prowess, are awesome.

◎ ◎ ◎ ◎

I've discussed only a few of the prominent contributors to women's surfing, and my focus was on competition champions. But surfing has a side that is quite distinct from competition. It's called soul surfing — surfing just to surf — and it focuses on the spiritual part of the sport. Women who practice it are also an important part of the surfing tapestry, and they can be just as inspirational, if not more, to beginners and experts alike.

Rochelle Ballard, fearless charger ('90s-'00s)

Keala Kennelly

Mary Ann Hawkins
with surf buddies

PART VI

# BOARD
# MEETING

# 18. SURFBOARD SELECTION

Feel fortunate that we've come a long way since surfers had to ride babies like the ones on page 85.

Ancient boards were made of wood, weighed a ton, and since they didn't have fins, they were hard to steer. In the 1930s, Tom Blake put a fin on a board, and in the late 1950s, Hobie Alter and Gordon Clark invented the process for mass-producing the durable, lightweight boards like the one you'll soon be riding.

Before we examine your board, let's get the basic vocabulary down.

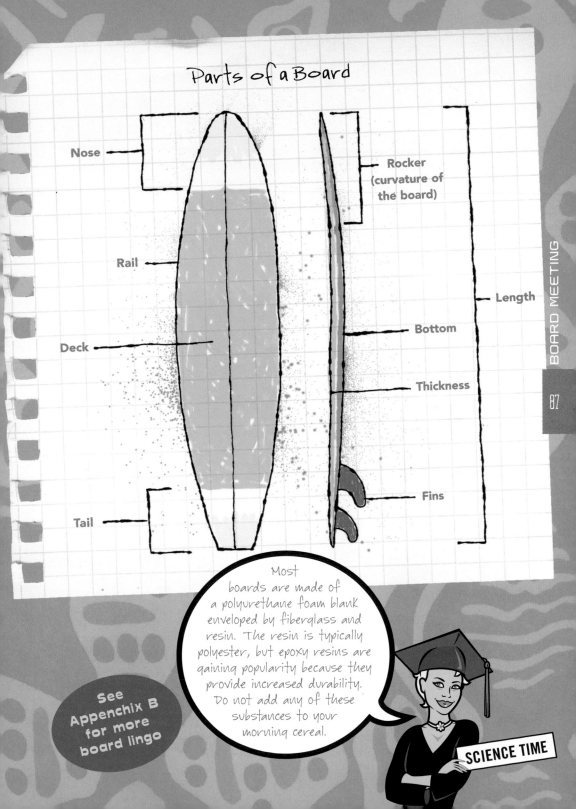

# Parts of a Board

Nose

Rail

Deck

Tail

Rocker
(curvature of
the board)

Length

Bottom

Thickness

Fins

Most boards are made of a polyurethane foam blank enveloped by fiberglass and resin. The resin is typically polyester, but epoxy resins are gaining popularity because they provide increased durability. Do not add any of these substances to your morning cereal.

See Appenchix B for more board lingo

**SCIENCE TIME**

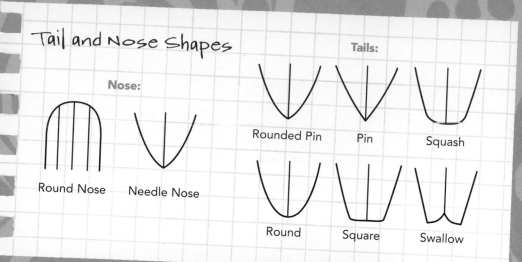

## Tail and Nose Shapes

**Nose:**

Round Nose

Needle Nose

**Tails:**

Rounded Pin

Pin

Squash

Round

Square

Swallow

## YOUR STARTING BOARD

People often get the idea that they'd like to start with a *shortboard* (a board under 7 feet) — it's easy to get impressed with the flicking snaps and radical movements you see some shortboarders make. But *longboards* (9 feet plus) have swooping arcs that are beautiful in their own right. It's actually an easy decision. You need as much wave time as possible at the beginning, and longboards and funboards (7 to 9 feet) will give it to you. How?

1. They provide more of a platform to stand on; you'll be more stable.

2. They have more surface area in contact with the water than a shortboard, making them easier to paddle.*

> \*The importance of paddling will be covered thoroughly in Section 21. Start loosening your shoulders now.

FOR THE **SPECS** ON YOUR STARTING BOARD, LET'S BRING OUT **DAIZE**...

IT'S TIME FOR HER TO REVEAL HER **SECRET**, THOUGH IT'S NOT REALLY **MUCH** OF A SECRET.

DAIZE SHAYNE ISN'T JUST ONE OF MY OLDEST **FRIENDS**...

SHE'S A TWO TIME WORLD **LONGBOARD** CHAMPION! WHO BETTER TO TALK ABOUT LONGBOARD SELECTION?

**Daize**

When selecting a longboard or funboard to start on, the rule of thumb is simple: get a big, heavy board. All you need to know at the very beginning are some basic specs:

- ◎ Over 7 feet in length
- ◎ 20 to 23 inches wide
- ◎ 1.5 to 3 feet taller than you
- ◎ Medium rocker

A funboard operates like a longboard to a kid or someone not particularly tall. As you progress, you can look closer at these characteristics:

## Length, Width, Thickness, Weight

As each characteristic increases in size (or weight), you'll float better, paddle easier, and catch more waves. The downside is the board tends to get less maneuverable.

## Rocker, Rails, Fins

**Rocker** is helpful because you'll be less likely to **pearl.** Pearling is where the nose of the board submerges, the board stops, and usually you wipe out. It's very common for beginners. The downside of a lot of rocker is that the board is harder to paddle.

**Rails?** Don't worry about it for now, but for your information, turned-down rails make the board easier to turn but less stable, while more rounded rails create more stability; you'll go slower and the board will be harder to turn.

**Fins?** Just make sure there's at least one.

As your surfing improves, you can move to boards with smaller dimensions and get more speed and maneuverability. You can even move into the shortboard world.

# Rent, Borrow, or Buy? New or Used?

For your initial sessions, renting a soft-top board is a good idea (cost: about $15–$20 per day, although some places charge $15–$20 per hour). A soft-top will help prevent bruises and cuts, since beginners invariably get in the way of their accelerating boards.

As soon as you learn some of the basic surfing skills, consider buying a used board (cost: about $75 to $300 for something decent). Your board will take abuse at first and you should minimize the cost profile of repairing and/or replacing it (new board cost: $450–$600 and up). Also, as you improve, you might prefer a different-size board than the one you did your basic learning on, so save some money on your short-term board.

Borrowing a board is a temporary scenario. Your cool friends will probably be fine with loaning you one, but part of being a surfer is owning and caring for your own. And besides, your potential to *ding* (cause a crack or break in the fiberglass skin) a board as a beginner is high, and no one likes their boards dinged, regardless of how gracious they are in loaning it to you. When you decide you want to follow through and learn to surf, buy yourself a stick.

# Buying a Board

When you're ready to buy, you have to consider the board's most important characteristic: does the color flatter your complexion? Relax, I'm joking. (That was for my friends who have actually mentioned this to me. C'mon, girls.)

**Used-board considerations:** Run your hands all over the board to make sure it's not waterlogged (feel for soft spots) or delaminating (notice if fiberglass is peeling away from the core). Avoid boards that are full of repaired dings. Remove the wax to check the condition of the deck.

**New-board considerations:** Try out a bunch of different-size boards before you fork out big cash. You're better off for resale value with a good brand name, and that applies to a used board, too.

# Board Care and Preparation

1. **No dinging.** Be careful not to bang your board into anything; it has a coat of fiberglass, which is a type of glass, and breaks like glass.

2. **Buy a board bag.** The sun damages boards by penetrating the fiberglass surface and making the foam core brittle. You'll notice it when the foam core starts yellowing. It reduces the life of the board. So don't leave your board sitting around in the sun. When you've finished a session, rinse off the salt water and sand and bag it.

3. **Wax on.** A good wax job is crucial. It'll help you stay on the board — thus allowing more wave-riding time — and minimize the opportunity for the kinds of injuries that result from slipping off the board (muscle strains, bruises from landing on the board, etc.).

# How To Wax A Board

1. **Buy wax.** First waxing? For a longboard, you'll need two bars of base coat and two bars of top coat. Top coat wax comes in different types based on the temperature of the water you'll be surfing in. Ask any local about the water temperature and check the wax wrapping for details. Some people like to store their wax in the fridge to keep it cool, which is fine, but could lead to an embarrassing moment if a guest attempts to include a wedge in their tuna-salad sandwich.

2. **Remove any old wax on the board.** Let the sun work for you.
   - Spread out newspaper in the sun. Put board on the paper, deck-up.
   - 20 minutes later, use cardboard to scrape off melted wax.
   - If you want every remnant of the old wax off, you can use a surf wax–stripping compound. If you use stripper, wash the deck off with water and dry it before waxing.

3. **Find a cool spot protected from the sun.** Make sure the board is on a forgiving surface (grass, a pad, your thighs, etc.), since you don't want the bottom scraped as you apply pressure on the deck.

4. **Apply the base coat.** Spread a light film across the entire ridable portion of your board, which, in the case of a longboard, is the whole deck. Just slide the bar lightly back and forth. After you've covered the deck with a film, start moving the bar in small circles. Build some *beads* or *bumps* — these little guys are the key to keeping your feet stuck to your board. Move all around the board and bump the whole surface up. The base coat process could take a good 10 or 15 minutes, but it's worth it.

5. **Apply the top coat.** Grab your top coat wax and work the bar in tight circles. For a longboard, wax from nose to tail and then from rail to rail (but not *on* the rails), and diagonally, too. If the wax smears, rotate the bar and keep circling. Surfboards are waxed wherever your feet may end up, and that means you can bump up the whole deck of a longboard.

6. **Combing.** Drag a wax comb across the board, length-wise, then diagonally and rail to rail, to create some grooves on your bumps.

7. **Keep wax off the bottom of your board.** It creates drag. Check it before going into the water.

Total elapsed time, including cleanup, is 20 minutes if you're quick about it.

# 19. ACCESSORIZE LIKE A MANIAC

- **Soft-Edge Fins** will reduce the chance of your getting cut if (or when) a fin hits you. Hard fins can be very sharp and a serious hazard. When I was ten, I came up after a wipeout and got a rude surprise. My board had been lifted by the wind and shot back into my forehead like a missile, fin-first. The result: ten stitches, seven across and three deep. No, I was not protecting my head and face upon surfacing like I should have been.

*My mom in her surf shop in the '80s.*

Need more evidence? A beginner friend of mine, actress Mara Lane, cut her foot on her fin, got twelve stitches, and it kept her out of the water for a month. She now swears by soft edges.

**WARNING:
Gross Photo
Ahead**

Here's more of Mara. These fins will not diminish your surfing experience; in fact, proponents argue that soft-edged fins actually give more control on turns since there's less turbulence around the fin. They also say these fins are closer to what dolphin and shark fins are like. Surfing like a dolphin is a very nice goal.

If you stay with hard fins, at least look for a board that has the fin edges dulled. If it doesn't, a shaper or repair specialist can sand them down for you. It won't eliminate the danger, but it might help reduce the severity of injury.

- **Leashes.** Get a leash at least as long as your board to improve the chances that it will clear you when you two become separated. The negative of long leashes is that there's extra work to retrieve the board after you fall, and that while you're trying, the board might be dragging you toward the shore. Better that, though, than having a leash that's too short; that will leave you more likely to collide with a board when you fall off and get churned.

  The leash strap should be affixed to the ankle of your back leg, not your front leg (and not around your neck!). Always wear it in the water.

  Make sure you tie the leash string close to your board; if it's left long it can wrap around the tail, and the force of a wave can send it through your tail (which would severely damage your board).

  Practice reaching down and ripping your leash's Velcro fastening off. It's rare, but a board or leash can get caught on something (like reef) and hold you under. Use two hands; if you use one hand in crunch time and fail, you might not have time to try two.

- **Traction pads** come in spray-on and stick-on varieties and eliminate the need for wax where you place them (although you should wax around them). They're commonly used on the tails of short boards and less often used on longboards. Note that they can rub and irritate the skin, particularly on the knees and chest.

- **Booties.** Used in cold water, depending on your tolerance, booties also will protect your feet from cuts and bruises. They may feel awkward at first, but you'll get used to them.

- **Webbed Gloves.** No, Aquagirl!

- **Helmets.** You can wear one if you want, but they're usually only used in big, dangerous surf with reef. Helmets can increase drag, however.

- **A Big Plastic Container.** You've performed a flawless surfer's change and now you're holding a soaking-wet wetsuit. Wrapping it in a towel won't work very well. Most hardware, drug, or discount stores sell plastic bins. Don't forget to remove your wet items from your car or the whole car will end up stinking.

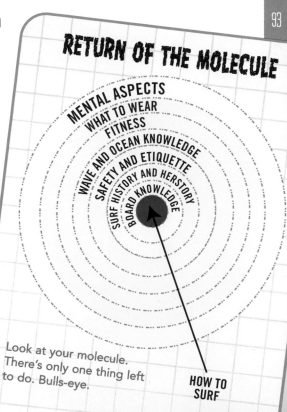

**RETURN OF THE MOLECULE**

MENTAL ASPECTS
WHAT TO WEAR
FITNESS
WAVE AND OCEAN KNOWLEDGE
SAFETY AND ETIQUETTE
SURF HISTORY AND HERSTORY
BOARD KNOWLEDGE

Look at your molecule. There's only one thing left to do. Bulls-eye.

HOW TO SURF

Just like the story of the origin of surfing, the triumphant story of your learning to surf will play out in three acts, and the scenes are right there in the surfer's molecule. We just need to zoom in closer.

**MENTAL ASPECTS**
**WHAT TO WEAR**
**FITNESS**
WAVE AND OCEAN KNOWLEDGE
SAFETY AND ETIQUETTE
SURF HISTORY AND HERSTORY
BOARD KNOWLEDGE

# HOW TO SURF

**ACT I**
Prep
Paddle
Sit 'n' Spin
Pop Up, Fall
Catch Mush

**ACT II**
Get Outside
Positioning
Catch a
Breaking Wave
Angle

**ACT III**
Trim
Cross-Step
Turn
Safety

**ACT I** is your call to adventure — it's about learning the basics for your journey into surferdom. **ACT II** is the part of the story where there are some trials and tribulations, but you overcome the difficulties and accomplish your primary goal of wave riding, and get revved up for the big finish. **ACT III** is where you solidify your skills and become a surfer who can adjust to the action of the waves, which is a most beautiful thing. One, two, three. Who said surfing was hard?

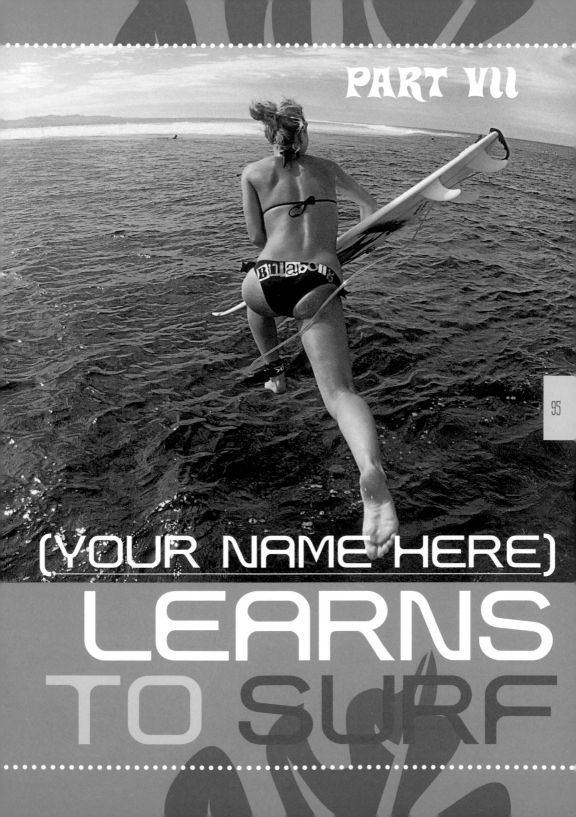

PART VII

95

(YOUR NAME HERE)

LEARNS

TO SURF

# 20. PREP

## ATTITUDE

Fold yourself into a sitting yoga-style position and say the following out loud five times: I am going to suck at the beginning, and it is okay.

Then say: I will improve as I practice, I will learn how to surf, and I will laugh at myself and have fun.

Now you're golden.

Leave your pride and ego on the beach. No cute surfer guy is going to be ripping up waves judging you and wondering why you can't surf. He knows why; all experienced surfers know why. They can spot a beginner all the way back in the parking lot. Yet, as long as you're respectful, no surfer cares that you're not a good surfer, because, frankly, all surfers have been there. We have all sucked. But we stayed with it, and now we don't suck.

Feel free to apply the "it's okay to suck at the beginning" philosophy to anything in your life (except skydiving).

*You HAVE to let pride go in order to make room to ABSORB life.*

## GETTING MENTAL, PART II

I harken back to Section 1: as you learn to surf, you develop a bundle of traits and skills, and as your bundle comes together at each level, you'll be prepared to progress to the next level. So, another trait you'll need is patience. Learning to surf is best done step by step. If you try to advance too quickly — beyond your abilities — you increase your chances for frustration and injury. Be tenacious, but don't rush.

Yeah, I used the word _harken!_

## SWIM, KIM

This may sound really obvious, but I need you to promise me you'll learn how to swim well. There was a time when there were no leashes and surfers had to be very good swimmers. Now, I see people in the water who depend on their leashes, and that's a bad idea. Leashes break, and when they do, your board will likely separate from you. It's happened to me several times far from shore. If I weren't a good swimmer, I would have been in serious trouble.

   Never surf anywhere that you can't easily swim to shore from if you get separated from your board.

## Ocean Swimming

Learning to swim for surfing also means taking time to swim in the ocean. Wave play will provide crucial lessons in how the ocean, waves, and currents work, and you'll start to develop your *feel*, which is important when it comes to catching and riding waves.

Wave play will also teach you how to keep yourself relaxed while being churned and thrown around. Avoid taking the brunt of the wave's energy (by ducking under them, for example). Tuck yourself into a ball, protect your head with your arms, and avoid collisions with the ocean floor. Two warnings: 1. Be careful in shorebreak — the explosive waves that crash close to the beach. Even small shorebreak can be powerful, and unaware swimmers regularly get slammed to the sand and hurt. 2. If you attempt to bodysurf, remember to always travel at an angle to the wave and shore. Don't go straight toward the shore; it's easy to get dumped on your head that way. People have broken their necks bodysurfing.

**Legal Liability Transferred Completely to Reader**

## Currents

Currents can be dangerous even when the waves are small. Being overly cautious is the way to go. Always swim where lifeguards are present, and ask them if there are strong or rip currents. Once, when I was five, I was swimming and I started to get pulled down the beach and out to sea. I was waving to my mom and yelling, and she smiled and waved back, not understanding. Luckily a couple of surfers were paddling in and they scooped me up. I've had the blessing of being able to scoop up a few swimmers myself.

Bottom line: when you go in, make it a point to tell the lifeguards where you are going to surf or swim. Surfers aren't immune — they occasionally get sucked out to sea with their boards and have to be rescued. Not only could that be a life-threatening situation, but it's *super-embarrassing*.

## STRETCHIN', GRETCHEN

For any sport, warming up will assist you in performance and injury prevention. This is particularly true for surfing, because the water will contort you into pretzel-like positions. Here are some suggestions:

◎ **Joint Mobilization.** Get everything moving. You can start with your fingers and work your way up. Rotate your wrists and arms; then get the shoulders going; then rotate at your neck, waist, and knees. Go clockwise, then counterclockwise. Lift each leg and give your ankles a spin.

◎ **Muscle Stretching.** With your arms stretched above your head, go back, forward, and to both sides. Stay in the extended positions, and let's impress Franz by breathing deep into the muscles.

◎ **Get Your Body Temp Up.** If it's really cold, do push ups, run on the sand, or maybe a few jumping jacks. Get creative and ignore the strange looks you'll receive. I'll tell you what I used to do in high school, but I wouldn't necessarily recommend it. Daize and I would roll up the windows of Daize's car, "Sam" (a blue Suzuki Samurai), and blast the heater. We'd also blast the music and scream along with the lyrics (usually punk stuff, like Pennywise or Rage Against the Machine). There was no good reason for doing this — the water is warm in Hawaii and the air temperature is usually at least 80. One thing's for sure, we *were* warmed up, and we always got a good laugh out of it.

Warm up complete? It's time to get in the water and have some fun. We'll start with four fundamentals: paddling, sit 'n' spin, popping up, and falling.

# 21. YOU'LL TAKE YOUR PADDLING AND LIKE IT

One of surfing's little secrets is that everything you need to do before popping up and riding a wave is probably more difficult than actually riding a wave. And "everything you need to do" will pretty much involve paddling.

## PADDLING OBJECTIVES

1. **Get to the Lineup.** The lineup is where surfers wait to catch waves. It's just outside of the breaking waves, and to get there you often need to push through incoming waves. Bad paddlers find themselves stuck inside, getting pounded. Their arms get tired and they can't move. They put their faces down and they lie flat on their boards like a lump of tuna. Good paddlers, on the other hand, zip out and set up for the next wave.

2. **Get into Position.** Once you're out in the lineup, you'll need your stroking to get you to the spot where you catch the wave. The better you are at paddling, the more waves you'll catch. A superior paddler spends more time riding waves because she paddles into position efficiently. A poor paddler wastes a lot of time and energy trying to catch, yet *just* missing, waves.

3. **Launch into the Wave.** Finally, you'll need some sprint paddling to create enough speed so you can properly merge with the wave as it begins to break. A few hard strokes should give you sufficient momentum, and away you go.

# HOW TO PADDLE

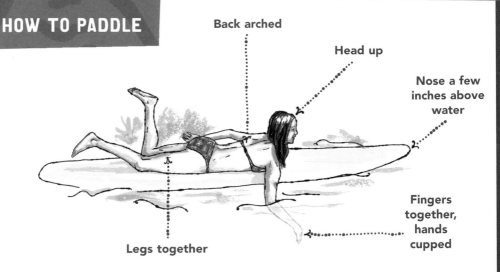

**Back arched**

**Head up**

**Nose a few inches above water**

**Fingers together, hands cupped**

**Legs together**

1. **Your Position Relative to the Board.** Efficient paddling begins with positioning yourself properly on the board. Facedown, centered (relative to the sides), and weight distributed so the nose of the board is a few inches above the water. If you're too far back, the board won't coast smoothly. Too far forward and the nose will dig in — possibly causing you to slip off the board.

   You're in the right position when you feel the board travel smoothly in the water and you feel yourself gaining momentum with your strokes. This is called gaining **trim**. You want trim; trim is your friend. If there's a design on the deck of the board, line your eyes up with it as a reference point for your best positioning.

   Also, keep your legs and feet on the board. It will prevent drag from extra limbs dangling in the water.

2. **Your Position Relative to You.** Back arched, head up, smile on your face. This will be difficult at first. Slowly you'll gain strength. Some people like to bend their legs; if it's comfortable, go for it. Keep everything still except your arms.

3. **Hands and Arms.** Keep your fingers together and form your hand into a spoon. Dig into the water on the down stroke and pull through hard. Pull even harder as your hand exits the water. Some people like to use an S-stroke while the hand is in the water. Experiment to see if tracing an S moves you faster. If not, forget it and just dig, baby.

Don't be surprised if you get tired fast and your arms noodle at the beginning. You'll be fine after 20,000 or so strokes.

# 22. SIT 'N' SPIN

Fundamental number two is going from a sitting position on your board — where you're perched, watching the incoming waves — to a prone position paddling into a wave to catch it.

## SITTING

At first, when you sit on your board, it will feel unsteady. Scoot yourself around until you're balanced. Position your board so it's pointed either directly at the horizon, parallel to the shore, or somewhere in between — whichever provides you with the best view to monitor the incoming sets while still allowing you to be aware of the surfers around you. There's an expression — it was one of the first things my dad taught me about surfing — "Don't turn your back on the ocean." It's truly is an invitation for a pounding. Big waves sometimes arise out of nowhere and you don't want to be blindsided.

After getting a feel for sitting, it's time to learn the spin.

## SPINNING

The following steps need to happen in rapid succession, because a wave might be getting ready to break.

1. Slide back on your board — let it tilt up out of the water — and grab the rail of the side you'll be spinning toward (with the hand closest to that rail).

2. Crank your legs like rotors, making fast, circular movements from the knees down.

3. Pull the rail in the direction you're spinning and paddle with the other hand.

4. Get into the prone position on the board. If you've picked a mark to line your eyes up with, you're ahead of the game and can get to a balanced position faster than if you were just guessing.

5. Start paddling.

# 23. POP-UP

A brief note of congratulations: you can paddle to where the waves are and you can spin and paddle into a wave. That's really good and it should make you want to dance.

Now you're ready for fundamental number three, the pop-up, which is what gets you from the prone position to standing and riding a wave.

## YOUR STANCE: REGULAR OR GOOFY?

Which foot should be forward when you jump up onto your board? There are a few ways to determine this:

1. Get on your stomach and pop yourself up like a surfer would. Whichever foot you naturally place as your front foot is likely to remain your front foot.

2. Which foot would you use to propel yourself when using a skateboard? That foot will usually, but not always, be your back foot for surfing. For everyone I know it is, but for me, it isn't. My right foot is back for skateboarding and my left for surfing. Weird, I know.

3. Figure it out in the water. You might switch back and forth to determine which feels most comfortable.

If your front foot is the left, you're a **regular** (or **natural**) footer. If you're front foot is the right, congratulations — you're a **goofy** footer.

regular

goofy

## THE REST OF YOUR STANCE

Two of the most common errors made by beginners is standing too straight and keeping their feet too close together. Let's avoid that.

### Feet Positioning

Your back foot is perpendicular to the stringer and your front foot is at a 45-degree angle pointing forward. Some surfers like to have the front foot almost parallel to the back foot — that's your choice. Your back foot will be above your fins and the front foot about shoulder-width forward.

Through trial and error in the water, you'll discover your *sweet spot*. That's the spot that allows the optimal maneuvering of your board. That's where you want your feet to be.

### Body Positioning

Crouch down and keep your back straight; you'll maintain your balance better. You've probably noticed how martial artists get down low so they're harder to knock over. Well, waves can hit a lot harder than martial artists. The thing I find myself yelling most often to my beginner friends in the water is, "Stay low, stay wide!"

Practice holding your stance at home: get low, get wide, and put your arms out for balance. Gaze proudly into the mirror if you like.

## THE POP-UP

Okay, you know how to stand on your board, so now we need to backtrack to get you into that position. The **pop-up** is done in one fluid movement. It's a push-up plus a sweep of your legs, followed by a planting of your feet into position.

### Push-Up

Place hands one hand-length south of where you'd put them for a regular exercise-style push up. This allows for your feet to land in the right spot when you pop up. If your hands are too far forward on the push-up, the feet often land too far back, resulting in your teetering forward — back bent — attempting to gain balance.

Your hands should be flat on the board; don't push up from a rail grab because if your hands slip, you might end up testing your board strength with your chin.

## Leg Sweep and Landing

As you push up, sweep your legs through — knees first — and rotate your lower half. Your objective is to land with your preferred foot forward, and your feet in surfing position (generally, perpendicular to the length of the board).

It's that simple — or, I should say, it *looks* that simple.

## PRACTICING POP-UPS

A lot of beginners pop up onto one knee before standing. Do not do that. Work on your strength and coordination at home with this exercise: from the prone position, put your hands into the pop-up position and pop up. Then do the reverse — a pop-down: lower yourself to the prone position as if you were doing the down portion of a push-up. To our weightlifting friends, this is called a negative, and it will build your strength.

Do 5 to 15 reps, but if you feel yourself slowing down, stop. The focus is on quality, not quantity. Do them wherever it is convenient, like while watching your favorite TV show; not only will it make the effort go by faster, it will provide substantial entertainment for your family and friends.

*Bonus exercise. Drop and give me 15, soldier.*

# 24. HOW TO TERMINATE YOUR RIDE WITHOUT MAIMING ANYONE, ESPECIALLY YOURSELF

You're almost ready to learn how to catch a ride. Before you do, though, you need to consider how you're going to end your ride. It's great if you can surf out the wave and casually return yourself to the prone position. More likely, though, you're going to eat it. It's an opportunity to hurt yourself that we will now help minimize.

## FALLING

1. Take a quick, deep inhale.

2. Jump away from the board.

3. Get your arms and hands around your head.

4. Lay into the water, flattening yourself out, as if you were plopping onto your sofa.

5. While being churned, tuck yourself into a ball and keep your arms around your head. The tuck is important because sometimes you don't know which way is up when you're getting churned, and you may be headed toward the ocean floor.

6. As you surface, put your arms or a hand in front of your face and protect your head. This is one of the most common times people get injured. Your own board may be lurking above you or others may be speeding toward you.

## DON'TS OF FALLING

**Don't be afraid of falling.** If you're afraid of falling, or failing, you may not even try. Practice falling. Embrace it. I love a good wipeout. It's cleansing.

**Don't dive head-first off your board.** It may look glorious to observers on shore, but your goal is to minimize, not maximize, the chances that your head will make contact with immovable objects. Don't think that deep water is necessarily safer for diving; there may be a reef around that you don't know about.

**Don't hop off your board in shallow water and land hard on your feet.** There are too many hazards: rocks, holes, uneven sand, and stingrays, to name a few.

## COMPLICATING FACTORS

### Other Surfers

Here's where the "without maiming anyone" part of the equation comes into play. If there are surfers around you or in your riding path, choose from the following:

1. If it's too crowded, let the wave go. There will be another.

2. If your fall is controlled, get a hand on your board. Be careful not to grab or make hard contact with your fin. Also, do not yank your shoulder out of its socket.

3. In stronger surf, where it's difficult to control your board, you can yell a warning. Remember to get some post-yell air into your lungs before entering the water, and feel good about taking care of your fellow surfer.

### No Control

Sometimes you *will* go flying off your board completely out of control. The one thing you must do is in this case is to get your arms out in front of your head and face. Your head, neck, and back need to be protected. Always err on the side of caution and you'll greatly increase your chances for long-term surfing fun.

Ask Cameron Diaz. She came up after a fall and took someone's board to her face. Result: broken nose, and that's one valuable nose. Yours is too, so protect it.

NOW YOU TELL US!

# 25. CATCHING YOUR FIRST RIDE

You'll never forget the first time; it's a memory you'll always cherish. But enough about kissing . . . now it's showtime.

## WHERE TO CATCH YOUR FIRST RIDE

Your first riding experiences should be at a sand-bottom break, usually called a **beach break.** The waves should be small and gentle and have lots of mellow, mushy, rolling white water *(soup)* on the inside. You're going to ride that mush.

Finding a spot where there are other beginners is a good idea, too, since the vibe will be mainly about learning. Just keep a lookout for errant boards; they tend to be shooting all over the place.

## WATER ENTRY

When you wade into the ocean, keep your board to the side of you and at a 90-degree angle to the waves — point it straight into the waves. Any deviation will likely get the board turned and launched toward the shore. If you're in the path of the board, expect a painful collision to your arm, chest or head.

## SET UP AND RIDE

1. Set up about 20 feet inside of where the waves are breaking. If the water is shallow, some beginners like to stand, but it's best to get used to sitting as soon as possible.

2. As the surging white water approaches, spin toward shore and get into the proper prone position. If you're too far forward, you might cause the board to pearl. If you're too far back, you might miss the wave. Keeping your back arched helps prevent pearling, too.

3. Start paddling. Turn your head and check repeatedly at the location of the wave — it's not essential for mush riding because proper positioning relative to the wave is not crucial, but you should get in the habit for when you surf breaking waves. You're also looking left and right for other surfers.

4. As the white water gets within 10 feet of you, employ your sprint paddling. Build your paddling speed before takeoff to match the speed of the wave. You need to merge with the wave. It often takes a few more strokes than you might have thought it would.

5. Feel the wave catch and accelerate you.

6. Pop up to your feet and take your stance.

7. Ride the wave.

8. Revel in the glory.

Congratulations! You really will remember this moment forever.

### Alter Your Direction

Repeat Steps 1 to 6 above, and when you ride the white water, try shifting your weight slightly to alter your direction to the left and right. Yes, it's almost a turn, but hold your horses, we'll pick up with the concept of angling and turning later. Okay, you can repeat Step 8 also.

### Find the Sweet Spot

Experiment to find out where on your board your feet should be to provide you with perfect balance and allow you to maneuver your board.

# ACT I REVIEW

"A magical and stunning performance by (your name here). She learned to swim like a mermaid and came to understand the ways of breaking waves by playing around in the ocean. She practiced the fundamentals with vigor, patience, and a great big smile on her face: she paddled, she did her sit 'n' spins, she popped up, and she learned to fall as safely as possible. All that, and she remembered to keep her head and face covered even upon emerging from a wipeout. *Bravo!* All in all, (your name here) clearly is absorbing the basics and is allowing them to become second-nature. She is now ready to proceed to the challenges of Act II, where she will be tested from head to toe and inside and out. She is realizing that she is indeed the heroine of this little story, and is starting to get used to it." — *Sanoe Gazette*

THIS THREE-ACT STUFF HAS ME THINKING WE SHOULD GET A RESIDUAL OR SOMETHING.

CALLING OUR AGENT NOW!!

# ACT II
## A SURFER IS BORN

Woman does not live by mush-riding alone. It's time for you to bump up the thrill level, and you'll do it by riding a breaking wave. Paddling out to the waves, standing up on them, and then doing something with them is not easy, but then, it wouldn't be a good Act II if it were, now would it? It's "trials and tribulations" time, but hang tough and you'll be glad you did.

Step number one in breaking-wave riding is finding them.

## FINDING YOUR SPOT

The spot for your first breaking wave may well be the spot where you took your first ride. A sand bottom and gentle, spilling waves are preferable to those that draw up and crash harshly. Most point and reef breaks are unsuitable for beginners because the waves are often too powerful and there's the chance of getting bounced off the reef. Ask a local expert about your best options.

Remember, it's best to stick with waves no bigger than waist-high. It may not sound like much, but it's a different story when you're on your stomach looking up (or on your feet getting pitched). Also, don't surf alone. Use the buddy system.

Keala killin' it at one of her favorite spots

# 26. GETTING OUTSIDE

To ride a breaking wave, you first need to transport yourself to the area just outside of where the waves are breaking. This is getting outside (in Section 7, we used another definition of "outside": being further along the breaking part of a wave relative to another surfer). Sometimes it's easy and sometimes it's challenging. It depends on the location and the conditions.

Here's where your paddling training will pay off.

There are two basic scenarios in getting outside: finding a channel and pushing through. However you do it, keep this in mind: it's a bad idea to paddle out directly behind other surfers. They or their boards (or both) could easily be driven back on top of you. Get your own clear lane.

## FINDING A CHANNEL

A **channel** is a seam in the water where waves aren't breaking, or, as is often the case at a beach break, where the waves are breaking less than the surrounding area. It's usually water that's deeper than where the waves are breaking nearby. The best way to find a channel is to watch the path other surfers take to get to their set-up positions.

Reef and point breaks often have easy-to-locate and consistent channels. At beach breaks, however, the changing tide and the shifting sand cause channels to form, disappear, and reform elsewhere . . . from day to day or moment to moment.

## PUSHING THROUGH

**Pushing through** refers to getting through breaking waves. You want to push through with the least amount of effort possible. Observe the sets before entering the water. Count how many waves per set and estimate the time between sets. If you time it right, you'll be able to minimize the resistance you encounter from incoming waves. The set information will come in handy when you catch your waves, too, and I'll tell you how later.

### Up and Over
The easiest way to punch through is to avoid the "punch" part: just paddle up and over the waves.

Build your momentum. Timing and wave knowledge will influence your ability to execute this, so it might not come easy at first. Feel free to employ your rapidly developing powers of perseverance and discipline. If the wave starts breaking as you're going up the face and you can't get over it, grab the rails hard and brace your back and neck: punch through.

## Getting Through Broken Waves

If the wave has broken in front of you, you have four main options:

1. **Push-Up.** When the waves are tiny and white water is rushing toward you, do a push-up on your board and let the water go between you and your board.

2. **Rock 'n' Roll.** Scoot to the back, grab the rails tightly, and tilt the board up — sitting up as you do it. As the white water hits the bottom of the board, press the board into it. The water will naturally lift you up and a bumpy ride through the mush will follow.

3. **Turning Turtle.** If a wave is about to land on you, you can turnturtle: invert yourself and your board, get a tight grip on your rails, and make sure your body and head are underwater (or else you'll take the hit from the wave). Let your board absorb the hit instead. Turning turtle usually gets you dragged back toward shore, but that's a small price compared to taking a direct hit from a bomb.

4. **Bailing.** As a last resort, you can throw your board away from you (toward the shore) and dive under the wave before it crashes. This breaks the rule of maintaining control of your board, but you might get surprised by a big wave and feel you have no other options. Before you do this, make sure that no surfers are behind you, lest your board should mangle them. Develop the other push-through methods and save this for when you really need it.

In all four instances, you should return as quickly as possible to the prone paddling position, headed outside. The next wave is likely coming and you want to build your momentum. You might be tired, but keep going — there'll be time for rest once you get outside the surf zone.

# 27. CATCHING A BREAKING WAVE

Whatever it took to get to the outside, it was worth it. Now it's time to select a wave. You should consider riding waves at the end of sets; that way, you'll have fewer (or no) waves to deal with when you paddle back out. This can save a lot of energy.

You'll thank me later for that little tip.

Before we discuss the details of paddling into your wave and managing the take-off, we need to cover the most important ingredient of catching and riding a breaking wave.

## POSITIONING

Positioning is the skill that will allow you to take off at the right spot, which is **at the peak.** This is where the wave begins breaking or curling. Taking off from the peak allows you to claim a wave — do you recall the main rule of surfing? — and is also ideal because it sets up your ride in the **pocket,** which is the area just ahead of the breaking portion of the wave.

The reason you want to be in the pocket is because that is where you can travel the fastest, Ms. Speed Demon.

Here's the thing: anticipating and locating this spot is something all competent surfers can do, but it can be frustrating to learn. Besides time-honed experience in the water, the keys to successful positioning are:

◎ **Observation.** Before you enter the water, take note of where the shortboarders and longboarders are setting up and taking off from. Read the waves and see if there are spots they are missing.

◎ **Landmarks.** When you're on the water, mark your takeoff positions with landmarks on shore. Use immovable objects such as a lifeguard station or a tree. If you can find landmarks on your left and right also, you can triangulate, which might help you set up even quicker.

◎ **Guts.** Being in the right spot to catch a breaking wave involves a scary little thrill: when the wave rises up behind you, it seems like it might break on top of you. You'll have to get over this. Having guts is also important because you have to negotiate surrounding surfers to work yourself into the mix.

## PADDLE INTO THE WAVE

The method for paddling into a breaking wave is similar to that described for catching mush in Section 25, Steps 1 through 5: spin, get prone, start paddling, look back over your shoulder, keep your back arched, etc. There's one difference, though: you might need to adjust your position relative to the wave as it's forming to get yourself to the takeoff spot. Keep in mind that every wave is different and you need to be flexible.

### Speed and Aggressiveness

Just as with the mush riding, you'll likely need to paddle hard to match your speed with the wave's. As you merge with the wave, take a last look around for other surfers. If a surfer is closer to the forming peak than you and it appears that he or she has a good chance of making the wave, back off and wait for the next one.

If you are the closest to the peak, pursue the wave aggressively. Part of surfing is taking charge of waves that are yours. This is neither the time nor place to be shy.

### Don't Miss the Wave

There are two common ways you might miss a wave:

1. The wave passes underneath you. This indicates that you started too late or you're too far back on your board.

2. The wave breaks on top of you. This indicates that you started too close to the shore, you need to move further outside.

## TAKEOFF

The difference between taking off on a breaking wave versus that of mush riding is that now you'll be **making a drop.** You'll be headed at an angle down the face of the wave.

Sure, it's a lot more difficult to pop up and stand on the board when the board is tilted, but it's also a lot more fun.

Prepare for the shoot to open, downhill-racer girl.

After you feel the wave start to accelerate you, pop up as soon as possible. You'll have more control of the board going down the face of a wave if you're standing.

Ride the wave straight in toward shore and repeat Step 8 from Section 25.

No worries if you find it hard to hit the right takeoff spot. Have fun with your failure; it's a brief stop on your way to success. You might even start too far inside on purpose and get pitched, just to get the feel of it. Why not take command of the learning process? Just remember to jump away from your board (review Section 24).

On the other hand, there's no shame in taking the first few rides all the way in on your stomach — it's still fun! Whatever it takes to get the feel of the waves is worth doing.

# 28. ANGLING

Riding waves straight in is a great start. Soon, though, you'll want more. **Angling** (*lala* to the ancient Hawaiians) brings the surfer to another level, since it allows you to maximize your speed and extend the length of your ride. Two wonderful things!

## GETTING LALA

The easiest way to ride a wave at an angle is to angle your takeoff (as opposed to dropping down and turning — you'll learn that soon). Point your board in the direction the wave is breaking and let the wave do the work — if it's breaking right, angle to the right. When you feel the wave catch you, pop up and get into your hot little stance. Ride as far as the wave will let you.

## FRONTSIDE, BACKSIDE

If you're a regular footer, going right will probably feel easier because you'll be facing the wave (your frontside). Going left, you'll have your back to the wave (backside). It's the opposite for goofy footers, of course. Frontside usually feels more natural at the beginning, and also allows for easier viewing of the wave characteristics in front of you. Over time, you'll need to be good going both left and right, so make sure to practice both.

Take some time out to celebrate (with moderation, of course); you really deserve it. Look how far you've come:

# HOW TO SURF

**ACT I**
✔ Prep
✔ Paddle
✔ Sit 'n' Spin
✔ Pop Up, Fall
✔ Catch Mush

**ACT II**
✔ Get Outside
✔ Positioning
✔ Catch a Breaking Wave
✔ Angle

**ACT III**
Trim
Cross-Step
Turn
Safety

## GOING FOR THE GOLD

## 29. TRIMMING

## THE IMPORTANCE OF TRIM

Once you're angling on a wave, a primary goal is to maintain trim — to keep your board gliding along as smoothly as possible. You know the feeling now; you felt it when you were paddling, when the waves accelerated you before you popped up, and when you rode the waves. You want to stay in touch with that beautiful feeling.

To maintain trim, you'll have to shift your weight distribution on your board. The reason? The wave will be applying its own forces on the board, which should be interpreted as a request for you to adjust. You must react. Sometimes it means applying pressure with either foot, or, as is more likely in the case on a longboard, you'll have to move yourself forward or backward along the board.

Properly responding to the wave's energy by adjusting your position on the board and/or the board's position on the wave is a Hallmark moment. You'll feel it from the tips of your toes to the top of your head.

## HOW TO MAINTAIN TRIM

The method for maintaining trim is something you might well do instinctively:

**When the board is starting to slow or stall, move (or apply pressure) forward. When the board is starting to pearl, move (or apply pressure) back.**

Just like when you were paddling, your objective is to keep the nose of the board coasting a few inches above the water. That's the position that will give you trim and keep the board moving fast. Your ideal location on the wave will be just ahead of the curl and probably on the upper third of the face.

### How to Move

There are a few ways to move on your board and skipping doesn't count. If a short move is required, a quick shuffle is fine. For longer moves, you need to learn another fundamental. You'll find it in the next section.

# 30. CROSS-STEPPING

Cross-stepping is the most efficient way to transport yourself along on a longboard.

Dance time. The cross-step should be performed fluidly — avoid hopping. Here's where chick surfers rule because it can look so darn graceful when a girl is moving up and down her board. The cross-step is simple. You're in your stance, your knees are bent, and you feel the board starting to stall (slow down), so you:

**Daize**

1. Bring your back foot across your front foot and as it starts bearing weight (your legs are now forming an X)

2. Bring the back foot across (behind) and plant it.

*Cha cha.* It's a two-step move. Your feet remain perpendicular to the stringer. Common mistakes I see are hesitating in the middle or moving too slow. Once you know you're going to cross-step, do the whole movement and do it fast. And *stay low.*

Daize keepin' it real

Now you're about halfway up your board. You might be done. See how your trim is. If it still feels like you're stalling, move forward. If you feel you're starting to dig in on the front or you want to slow down, move back. Do that by taking a short shuffle, or reversing the cross-step process:

1. Front foot crosses behind back foot and plants.

2. Front foot crosses in front of back foot and plants.

EASY HUH?

YOU CAN **PRACTICE** THE CROSS-STEP AT HOME, TOO!

YOUR FAMILY AND FRIENDS ARE WAITING FOR YOU TO TOP YOUR POP UP EXHIBITIONS FROM SECTION 23 AND HERE'S YOUR CHANCE!

# 31. TURNING

A turn is used to set up a maneuver or reposition you in the wave. When repositioning, the goal is usually to get yourself into the pocket. How wide or sharp you make your turns will be dictated by the wave.

*Keala doing damage*

## TYPES OF TURNS

The three most common turns are the **bottom turn,** the **top turn** (made in the upper portion of the wave), and the **cutback.** The **kickout** is a slick and useful turn that carries you up and out of the wave when you've completed your ride. It's great for avoiding close-outs. We'll illustrate the bottom turn. It's the next step for you after you've made your drops and ridden waves straight in, and it is the most fundamental of the turns.

## HOW TO TURN

Turning a longboard takes more planning and space than turning a shortboard. We'll present it in three steps, but the steps happen fast; practically at the same time.

1. **Position Your Feet.** Plant your feet and prepare to turn. Your back foot *needs to be planted at the tail.* The experimenting you've done to find the sweet spot on your board will pay off now. If you're too far forward when you attempt a turn, you'll likely *dig a rail* (jam the edge of the board in the wave) and a wipeout will likely follow. If you're too far back, you'll lose speed and might even spin out.

2. **Look to the Spot.** Just as you're preparing to turn, focus on your destination.

3. **Shift Your Weight.** Bend your knees and lean your weight in the direction you want to go — toward your toes if you want to turn forward; back on your heels if you're turning backside. To sharpen the angle of the turn, crouch and use torque as needed. Feel those glutes getting worked!

The key is to think *smoothness* and allow the energy of the wave to inform you about where the board should be. Sounds mystical, I know. Well, welcome to surfing.

## WHEN TO TURN

Every wave is different. Turn too soon and you'll turn out of the wave. Turn too late and the curl might pass you by. Only experience will help.

## AFTER TURNING

After you turn, and after you've positioned yourself in the pocket, you'll often find yourself needing to adjust your position on the board to maintain trim. Revisit the cross-stepping section for directions on what to do next.

As fun as it was just to ride the mush and make the drop, executing a bottom turn and slipping into a pocket is a whole new level of joy.

# 32. THE PRIZE

In every good adventure, the hero brings back something special to show his or her loved ones. A prize, or perhaps some special information. In your case, it's both. The prizes include knowing how to surf, and, I hope, a tighter connection with nature and a higher level of confidence gained by developing your courage, perseverance, discipline, focus, and respect.

Your special information includes the safety information that will keep you as healthy as possible while you surf.

I decided to put the safety tips in one place so you could easily refer to them. Please review these until you don't have to think about them and they just become part of you. It really could be the difference between your taking that one hard hit to the head that you wish you hadn't, or worse.

## SAFETY TIPS

1. First, become a good swimmer in the ocean. Never surf in a place that you couldn't *easily* swim to shore from if you were separated from your board.

2. Surf and swim at beaches with lifeguards and ask them about local reef and current conditions.

3. Maintain awareness — know where surfers are all around you.

4. Do not let your board get between the wave and you. Keep your board to the side of you or to the shore side of you.

5. Adhere to the main rule of surfing: the right of way belongs to the surfer taking off closest to the breaking part of the wave.

6. Don't be stingy with the water-resistant sunblock. Reapply.

7. Do not surf alone or in the dark.

8. Do not panic. Nasty wipeout? Caught in a rip current? Caught inside? Focus on the fact that there is a way out, and it's a lot easier to locate it if you stay calm.

9. When you fall off your board, cover your head and face and keep them protected when you eventually surface.

10. When paddling out, do not paddle out directly behind another surfer.

11. Surf only in waves that are comfortable for you to be in, in locations that are safe (preferably with a sand bottom).

12. Get soft-edge fins or make sure the edges of your fins are dulled.

13. Shuffle your feet when you're walking in shallow water — stingrays prefer not getting stepped on.

14. Do not attack sharks unless provoked.

15. Don't even attempt bigger waves or more complicated maneuvers until you've really mastered the basics.

16. Use your instincts. If something doesn't feel right, go with that feeling. Fast.

# ALOHA

I hope that if you try surfing, you experience even some of the joy I feel when I am on the water.

When I said that the ocean gets into your blood, I meant it figuratively, but it works on a literal level as well. Many beaches are already so polluted that you can't go in the water and the situation is only getting worse. Those who don't know the ocean may not yet understand the need to keep the oceans clean, but we surfers do, so it is our duty to get involved. Please review Section 15 and the resources available in Appendix C. We must work together to care for the ocean, for our sake and for the sake of the generations to come.

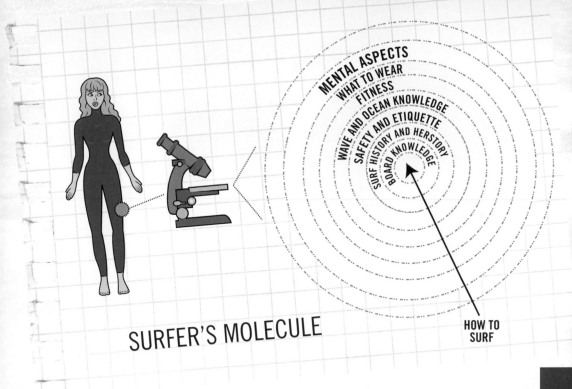

SURFER'S MOLECULE

MENTAL ASPECTS
WHAT TO WEAR
FITNESS
WAVE AND OCEAN KNOWLEDGE
SAFETY AND ETIQUETTE
SURF HISTORY AND HERSTORY
BOARD KNOWLEDGE

HOW TO SURF

With the molecules in your body transitioned, maybe you will carve out a new kind of life for yourself. I added a ring and left it blank. I'm sure surfing will provide you with opportunities to fill it in. Everyone finds his or her own things about the surfing experience that change them in some way. Maybe things I haven't even dreamed of.

Aloha is a Hawaiian word with many meanings, but mainly it's a spirit. It is that spirit I wish upon you as I say good-bye and wish you safe surfing, happiness, and success in all of your endeavors. God bless and aloha!

Love,

Sanoe

# APPENCHIX
## AND
## RESOURCES

## WAVE RIDING

### TURNS

#### THE THREE FUNDAMENTAL TURNS

**BOTTOM TURN** Turning at the bottom of the face of the wave. Fundamental step to setting up tube ride and other maneuvers.

**CUTBACK** Maneuver to take the surfer from the non-breaking part of the wave (shoulder) to the breaking part.

**TOP TURN** Turn made to re-enter wave after heading toward the top of face.

#### MORE TURNS

**DROP-KNEE** A method used to turn a longboard. Trail leg is bent inward, lowered toward the front foot. A bit showy.

**KICKOUT** Terminating the ride by sharply turning out the back of the wave before it fully breaks.

**SNAP** A sharp turn, generally executed off the lip. Also *snapback.*

### MANEUVERS

**AERIAL** The surfer and surfboard launch off a wave. Only impressive if you stick the landing. Also *air.*

**BACKDOOR** To pull into a tube from behind the peak. Also *backside.*

**CHEATER FIVE** Crouching surfer places the toes of front foot over the nose of a longboard. It's a "cheat" because weight remains on back leg.

**CHOP-HOP** Derogatory term for aerial performed in small surf.

**CROSS STEP** Technique for getting the surfer to the front or back of a longboard. One foot crosses the other, the legs form an X, and then the other foot crosses over.

**FLOATER** Advanced maneuver whereby surfer cruises the top of a broken wave, or the top of a curl, as if "floating."

**HANG TEN**  Ten toes are over the nose of the longboard.

**SOUL ARCH**  Chest out, back bent, to show mastery of wave. Performed while angling across a wave face, on a bottom turn, or in a tube. Arms may be raised over head, superstar.

**STALL**  Slowing a moving board. *Kick stall:* shifting weight toward back of board so front lifts up. *Arm stall:* drag arm in face of wave. *Delayed-turn stall:* slow, wide bottom turn.

**TAILSLIDE**  Surfer purposely makes her fins lose their grip and rides the board sideways or tail-first down the face of the wave.

**TOES-ON-THE-NOSE**  Riding a wave with one's toes curled around the nose of the board. Five, ten, or however many you want.

## WIPEOUT

**BAIL**  To abandon, or jump off, one's board while riding a wave.

**DIG A RAIL**  To bury the rail of the board beneath the surface of the water while riding a wave; often results in an abrupt slowing, followed by a nice wipeout.

**EAT IT**  To fall off board and get hammered by a wave.

**OVER THE FALLS**  Surfer gets sucked up into the wave and pitched with the curling lip. One of the most dangerous ways to wipe out.

**PEARL**  When the nose of the board submerges. Occurs most frequently upon take-off and usually results in the surfer going face-first over the front of the board. From "pearl diving."

**PITCHED**  Tossed off the wave and off the board.

**SLAMMED**  Wave lands on a surfer.

**STUFFED**  Getting driven under the water by a breaking wave.

**WORKED**  As in "getting worked," the action a wave and white water play on a surfer, much like being in a large washing machine.

## EXPRESSION SESSION

**AIR**  Result of an aerial, as in "getting some air."

**BARREL, TUBE**  The hollow part of a wave formed by the lip peaking and falling to the trough. Also, *green room, getting tubed, barreled* or *covered.* Usually formed when incoming waves hit a shallow area (sandbar or reef). Also *slotted, pitted.*

**BOOST**  Getting airborne off the lip while performing an aerial.

**BUMPS** Uneven buildup of wax on a surfboard deck.

**COMBER** Wave (ancient term).

**DING** A hole, dent, crack or scratch on a surfboard. Must repair to prevent seawater from seeping in and damaging the seal between the foam and fiberglass.

**GASH** Super-sharp turn. Also *gouge*.

**GLIDE** Term describing the motion of a board across the face of the wave.

**GUNNED** Usually as *undergunned* or *overgunned*. Refers to the size of your board in relation to wave conditions.

**LOCAL** A surfer known to frequent a particular break.

**LOCALISM** Surf behavior of locals, which is often hostile to visitors.

**LOG** Term used to describe an old board, sometimes heavy from taking on water.

**NOODLE** Refers to how surfers' arms might feel after an extended session.

**PACK** Crowd of surfers. Also *lineup*.

**PLANK** Longboard.

**SCABBED** Getting damaged by a reef or rock.

**SESSION** A period of time spent surfing.

**SHRED** Surf at a high level, tearing up a wave. Also *rip*.

**SICK** Refers to a maneuver executed to near-perfection.

**STICK** Surfboard.

**SURF'S UP** Yeah, whatever.

**TRIM** 1. Adjusting your position on a board so that it planes and achieves its maximum speed. 2. Achieving a smooth path along a wave face.

**VERTICAL** To turn and ride straight up the face of the wave.

## OFFENSIVE

**DROPPING IN** Taking off on a wave that another surfer — closer to the breaking part of the wave — is already riding. The biggest surfing sin. Also *cutting off*.

**SNAKE** Paddling behind someone who is in position and stealing his or her wave.

**KOOK** Annoying beginner or arrogant problem-causer.

**BACKSIDE**  Surfer rides with back to wave.

**DROP**  The initial downward slide on the face of the wave after taking off.

**DROP IN LATE**  Taking off on the steepest part of a wave after it has begun to curl.

**DUCK DIVE**  Technique used to get through breaking waves and out to the lineup; involves forcing your board underwater and ducking beneath the breaking wave, for the purpose of avoiding the brunt of the wave's energy.

**FRONTSIDE**  When a surfer rides facing a wave.

**GOOFY FOOTER**  Surfer who uses right foot as lead foot.

**HEAD DIP**  Surfer allows head to brush against the lip while getting barreled.

**POP-UP**  The act of going from a prone position to a standing position in one fluid motion.

**SIDESLIP**  When surfer's board stops tracking forward and moves sideways.

## LOCATION, LOCATION, LOCATION

**INSIDE**  The area of breaking waves closest to shore.

**CAUGHT INSIDE**  Surfer on the shore-side of breaking waves who is getting thrashed. Not the best place to be on larger days.

**LINEUP**  Surfers lined up in the water where the wave breaks, waiting to catch approaching waves.

**OUTSIDE**  A place in the lineup beyond where the waves are consistently breaking.

**TAKEOFF POINT**  The optimal spot to be in the lineup to catch the best part of a breaking wave.

## WAVE ACTION

**BACKWASH**  Flood of water returning off the foreshore against incoming waves. In some places it can be surfed, with caution.

**BOTTOM**  Referring to the ocean floor or to the lowest part of the wave.

**BOWL**  Shallow spot in the path of the wave, causing the wave to break a little harder.

**CHANNEL**  Deep spot where waves don't normally break; ideal for paddling back out to the lineup, as opposed to being "caught inside."

**CLOSE OUT**  When a wave breaks simultaneously across its entire width. Impairs the surfer's ability to both catch waves and paddle out to the lineup.

**CLEANUP WAVE**  Large set wave that breaks outside of the lineup, dumping on the entire lineup.

**CONSISTENT**  Term used to describe waves breaking in a similar fashion over an extended period of time.

**CRITICAL**  Describes the steepness and speed of break.

**CURL**  Breaking part of a wave.

**FACE**  Front part of the wave. The part you surf.

**IMPACT ZONE**  Point where the waves break for the first time inside; if it's big enough, where waves continue to break, reform, and break again. Minimize your time here. Also *death zone*.

**LIP**  Top of the face of the wave. Usually curling forward.

**MUSH**  Slow, sloppy waves of little power (still better than no waves). Also *mushburger.*

**PEAK**  Point of wave which first begins to break.

**PIT**  Most critical section of the wave; the section closest to the forming peak.

**POCKET SECTION**  Part of a wave, usually referring to a rideable portion that stretches ahead of the curling lip.

**SET**  Group of waves that break in a pattern.

**SHOREBREAK**  Waves that break very close to the beach.

**SHOULDER**  End section of breaking wave.

**SOUP**  Foamy white water produced by broken waves.

**STEEP**  Refers to angle or pitch of wave face.

**TUBE**  Cylindrical or cone-shaped hole created when the lip pitches out far and clean enough to create a space between the wave and the falls.

**WALL**  Unbroken face of a wave.

## CONDITIONS

**BLOWN OUT**  When high winds cause the surf to become choppy and unridable.

**BOMB**  Giant wave.

**BUMP**  Increase in swell.

**BUMPY**  Refers to choppy conditions affecting the wave face.

**CHOPPY**  Very small waves on the surface created by local winds.

**CLEAN**  Refers to glassy, non-closed-out conditions.

**EPIC**  The best conditions possible.

**GLASSY**  When there is no wind and the surface of the water becomes smooth.

**GOING OFF**  Describes large surf breaking under optimum conditions.

**OFFSHORE**  Winds blowing from shore to ocean; often makes for a clean wave and helps the curl hold up.

**ONSHORE**  Winds blowing from ocean to shore; puts ripple in surf, and if winds are strong, ruins surf.

**OVERHEAD**  Reference to the height of the face of the wave — it's taller than a surfer.

**PUMPING**  Refers to large waves accompanied by good conditions.

**SWELL**  Wave. Also, a system of waves coming.

### TYPES OF WAVES

**BEACH BREAK**  Waves breaking over a sand bottom, can shift seasonally and from storm to storm.

**GROUND SWELLS**  Waves formed over vast distances, well-formed and powerful.

**POINT BREAK**  Long, unvarying waves that usually break along a point that extends from the coastline.

**REEF BREAKS**  Wave is formed over an underwater reef or rock. A consistent break with consistent takeoff positions.

**RIVER MOUTH BREAKS**  Wave forms on the sediments deposited at the river mouth; similar to beach breaks, but sometimes more susceptible to change.

**WIND SWELLS**  Waves formed by wind. They tend to be sloppy and unorganized. Also *wind slop*.

# ATTITUDE

**DAWN PATROL**  Surfers who surf at sun up. Also *crackin' it*.

**GNARLY**  Intimidating.

**GROMMET**  Young surfer. Also *grom* or *gremmie* (from *gremlin*).

**HONEY**  A female surfer.

**SPONGER**  Affectionate term used by surfers to refer to boogieboarders. *Booger* to Aussies.

**STOKED**  Geared up, wound up, full of enthusiasm. Also *amped*.

## PLACES YOU SHOULD KNOW

**JAWS**  Maui. One slip and it could be over.

**JEFFREY'S BAY**  South Africa. Also, *J-Bay*.

**MAVERICK'S**  Santa Cruz, California.

**NORTH SHORE**  Northern part of Hawaii's most populous island, Oahu.

**PIPELINE**  One of the world's most dangerous breaks. Located on the North Shore of Hawaii, it is huge, unforgiving, and you get two waves in one: the left break is Pipeline, the right break is Backdoor.

**SNAPPER; KIRRA**  Both in Australia.

**TAVARUA**  Fiji.

**TEAHOPOO**  Tahiti. Another one of the world's most dangerous breaks. The waves there can be shockingly heavy . . . you gotta see it to believe it.

**THE BOX**  Washington State, United States.

# APPENCHIX B
# BOARD LINGO

**BLANK**  Polyurethane foam with thin wood strip molded into surfboard shape. It's the core material of a board.

**BODYBOARD**  A Hawaiian paipoboard originally modified in 1971 by Tom Morey to ride dangerous shallow reefs safely. Rider lays prone and augments his or her paddling speed and turning with swim-fins. Also *boogie board*.

**CONCAVE**  Indentation running lengthwise on the bottom of a board, believed to create lift. Also *spoon*.

**DECK**  Top of a surfboard.

**DING**  Scratch, dent, or gouge in a surfboard that needs repairing so water doesn't enter and ruin the foam core.

**EGG**  Refers to a particular surfboard shape, where the nose and tail are rounded.

**EPOXY**  Board that uses epoxy resin instead of polyester resin.

**FIBERGLASS**  The easily breakable skin of your board. It's a silica-based fabric.

**FIN**  Rudderlike appendage attached to bottom of board to facilitate turning.

**FUNBOARD**  Board ranging from 7 to 9 feet shaped to provide some of the floatation and paddling of a longboard plus the performance (turning ability) of a shortboard. Also *hybrid.*

**GUN**  A board used for riding big waves. They are long, narrow, and pointy both at the nose and the tail for maximum rail contact. Usually thick and heavy and ranging in length from 7 to 10 feet. Also called an *elephant gun* or *rhino chaser,* because you take it with you when you're hunting big game.

**HARD RAIL**  Sharper edge to grab a wave.

**KNEEBOARD**  Small board ridden in a kneeling position.

**LEASH**  Line attaching the surfboard to the rider's ankle, calf, or thigh, or, in the case of a bodyboard, his or her wrist.

**LONGBOARD**  Surfboard usually 9 feet or more in length.

**OUTLINE**  Refers to the outside shape of the board.

**PIN TAIL**  Pointed tail; aids in stability of board.

**QUAD** Four-fin board.

**QUIVER** A surfer's collection of boards.

**RAIL** Side edge of a board.

**ROCKER** Amount of curve in a surfboard from nose to tail; more rocker provides for easier turning but less speed.

**SHAPER** Person who creates surfboards.

**SHORTBOARD** Ranges in length from 5 to 7 feet and tends to be used for high-performance surfing.

**SKEG** Fin (middle fin if there are three).

**SKIMBOARD** Glassed plywood disc or oval for riding shorebreak on the water's edge. Run, throw it down, hop on, and steer into a wave.

**SOFT RAIL** Rounder edge so the board is looser.

**SPOON** Concave in the underside nose of a longboard. Increases lift for nose riding.

**STRINGER** The wooden piece running down the middle of the plank that gives it strength.

**SQUASH TAIL** Wide, rectangular tail, introduced after the advent of advanced fin systems to loosen the board up

**SWALLOW TAIL** Double pointed tail with an indentation in the center.

**TAIL KICK** An increase in the rate of rocker near the tail.

**THRUSTER** Three-finned board. Made popular by Australian shaper Simon Anderson. Also *tri-fin*.

**TWIN-FIN** Guess how many fins on the board.

**WAX** Used on deck of boards for traction.

For an in-depth look at boards, try *Essential Surfing* by George Orbelian. Read that book a few times and soon you'll be building your own boards.

# APPENDIX C
# RESOURCES

The resources listed below, like the other information in this book, is based upon sources that the authors believe to be reliable, and is current as of June 2004. All Web sites are *http://www* unless otherwise noted.

## GIRLS' SURF SITES

| | |
|---|---|
| **Sisters Of The Sea** | sistersofthesea.org |
| **Surfer Skater Snowboarder Magazine** | surfinggirl.com |
| **Surf Life For Women** | surflifeforwomen.com |
| **Trixie Surf** | trixiesurf.com |
| **Wahine Surfing** | wahinesurfing.com |

## INSTRUCTION AND SHOPS

### Western U.S., Mainland

| | |
|---|---|
| **Girl In The Curl Surf Shop** | Girlinthecurl.com |
| **Move Over Boys** | moveoverboys.com |
| **Paradise Surf** | paradisesurf.com |
| **Pink Lava Women's Surf Shop** | pinklava.com |
| **Surf Diva** | surfdiva.com |

### Eastern U.S.

| | |
|---|---|
| **Surfing In Rhode Island** | warmwinds.com |
| **East Coast Wahines** | eastcoastwahines.com |
| **Radical Slide** | radicalside.com |

### Hawaii

| | |
|---|---|
| **Honolua Wahine** | honoluasurf.com |
| **Maui Surfer Girls** | mauisurfergirls.com |
| **Surf Lessons By Margo Oberg** | surfonkauai.com |

### Australia

| | |
|---|---|
| **Women in Waves** | women-in-waves.com.au/ |

## FORECASTING AND MORE

| | |
|---|---|
| A1Surf - U.K. | a1surf.com |
| Boardfolio | boardfolio.com |
| Association Of Surfing Professionals | aspworldtour.com |
| Eastern Surfing Association | surfesa.org |
| Fluid Groove | fluidgroove.net |
| Freshwax | freshwax.com |
| Global Surf | globalsurf.com |
| Gumby Lock | gumbylock.com.au |
| NSSA | nssa.org |
| Surfline | surfline.com |
| Surfers Directory | Surfers-directory.com |
| Swaylocks | swaylocks.com |
| The Glide | theglide.com |
| Transworld Surf | transworldsurf.com |
| Wave Masters Society | wavemasters.org |
| Wet Sand | wetsand.com |

## HISTORY AND HERSTORY

| | |
|---|---|
| California Surf Museum | surfmuseum.org |
| International Surfing Museum | surfingmuseum.org |
| Legendary Surfers | legendarysurfers.com |
| Surf Style | surfstyle.org |
| Terry Tubesteak Tracy | tubesteak.org |

## ENVIRONMENT

| | |
|---|---|
| Coastal Cleanup | coastalcleanup.org |
| Envirolink | envirolink.org |
| Groundswell Society | groundswellsociety.org |
| Less Than One | lessthanone.org |
| Oceana | oceana.org |
| Marine Protected Areas | mpa.gov |
| Ocean Futures | oceanfutures.com |
| Surfers' Environmental Alliance | seasurfer.org |
| Surfrider Foundation | surfrider.org |
| The Ocean Project | theoceanproject.org |

## REGIONAL

| | |
|---|---|
| Clean Ocean Action (New York) | cleanoceanaction.org |
| Heal The Bay (California) | healthebay.org |
| Ocean Watch (Florida) | oceanwatch.org |
| Save Our Seas (Hawaii) | saveourseas.org |
| Sound Waters (New York) | soundwaters.org |
| Surfers Against Sewage (United Kingdom) | sas.org.uk |
| Tidepool (Northwest U.S.) | tidepool.org |

# HEALTH AND FITNESS

**Surfer's Medical Association**
PO Box 1210, Aptos, CA 95001
831.684.0916
SMACentral@aol.com
**Franz Snideman,** Strength and Fitness Training: Franzsnideman.com

# REFERENCE

The following books were used in researching this book. They are all good reads and will all expand your knowledge of surfing.

*Surfing: A History of the Ancient Hawaiian Sport* by Ben Finney and James D. Houston

*Girl in the Curl, A Century of Women's Surfing* by Andrea Gabbard

*Essential Surfing* by George Orbelian

*Longboarder's Start-Up* by Doug Werner

*Encyclopedia of Surfing* by Matt Warshaw

*How Fo' Surf (Wit' Palaka Joe)* by Patrick Ching and Jeff Pagay

Would you like to read an excellent short-story collection about surfing? I highly recommend Chris Ahrens' book, *Kelea's Gift*. The title story is based on the legend of a girl shredder from Maui — around 500 years ago — who was kidnapped because of her surfing prowess. It's available through www.chubascopublishing.com.

If you're interested in more detail about waves, try this book: *Waves and Beaches: the Dynamics of the Ocean Surface* by William Bascom.

# PHOTO AND ART CREDITS

Leroy AhChoy: 8 (middle)
Georgette Austria: 39
Larry Bartholomew: 36 (top), 55
Bishop Museum Archive: 19 (middle), 20, 22, 23, 26
© Brown & Bigelow, Inc.: 76 (painting by Duane Bryers)
Don Diaz: 27 (middle)
Jeff Divine: 77, 80 (lower left), 81 (top), 82 (top)
Michael Eaton: 30
N.R. Farbman, Bishop Museum Archive: 18-19 (top)
LeRoy Grannis: 78, 79 (top), 80 (top), 80 (right), 81 (lower right), 85 (that's LeRoy on
    the far right, circa April 1937)
Steven Jarrett: 29
Kalaea Lake: 144
Laola Lake: 8 (top), 9 (top and bottom), 46, 129
Sanoe Lake: 3 (bottom), 9 (middle), 17, 48, 49, 82 (right), 84, 89, 92 (top), 122
Mara Lane: 75, 92 (middle)
Milnor Pictures, Inc.: 8 (bottom)
Paul Naude: Front and back cover insets, back cover, 2, 86, 95, 97, 106, 113, 120
Scott Needham/SNP5000.com: Front cover, 5 (top), 57, 65, 128
Jessica Trent Nichols: 131

Mikel Roberts: 92 (lower right)

© Jim Russi/Photorussi.com: 50, 81 (bottom left), 83 (top and bottom), 110, 123

James Sartain: 19 (bottom), 47

Tom Servais: 4 (top), 11, 27 (right), 34 (top and bottom), 36 (lower left), 37 (bottom), 43, 45 (full page), 66, 72, 73, 82 (bottom), 96, 99

Daize Shayne: 82 (middle)

David Tsay: 3 (left and right), 24, 25, 27 (lower left), 28 (left and right), 32, 33, 35, 36 (lower right), 37 (top), 51, 54

Universal Pictures: 1, 4 (bottom), 6, 28 (bottom), 38, 45 (inset), 63 (all three), 100

Karen Wilson © ASP Karen: 5 (middle), 124

Kathy Kohner Zuckerman Collection: 79 (bottom)

## ACKNOWLEDGMENTS

**The authors would like to thank the following people for their generous assistance in the creation of this book:**

Andrea Spooner, Lisa Queen, Sophia Seidner, Cindy Kauanui.

**And:** Billy Hughes, Chris Ahrens, Daize Shayne, Keala Kennelly, Franz Snideman, Debbie Beacham, Laola Lake; Greg Mattson, MD; Michael Lauer, MD; Marie Kivett, Margo Oberg, Jericho Poppler, Tiffany Pixler, Mia Enriquez, Kathy Kohner Zuckerman, Jenn Hoffman; the folks at Bishop Museum Archives: DeSoto Brown, Ron Schaefer, Deanne DuPont, and Leah Caldeira; the crew at Billabong: Candy Harris, Amy Botts, Megan Brainard, Mandy Robinson, and Danielle Petach; Steve Steinman, Kurt Toneys, Frank Beacham, Rick Klune, Robin Bonaccorsi, Sanoe's surfboard sponsor, Spyder Surfboards, Christina Nguyen, Dylan Gerber, Peter Gerber, Jay Silverman, Anne Medcalf, Rachel Perris, Jae Hauser; Jeremy Laws and Roni Lubliner at Universal; Lindsay Stewart and especially Nicole Carrico at Jet Set; Lani Kuramoto, Sangeeta Mehta; our instructional illustration models: Leela Harpur, Mara Lane, Jess Cramp; Judy Harpur, Dion Becker, Denny O'Connor, Mitch's Surf Shop, Marshall Clark, Robert Earl, Amy Anderson, Brianna, and the one and only Ruby Universe.

**And a special thank you to the photographers who graciously allowed us use of their photos: Larry Bartholomew, Jeff Divine, Don Diaz, LeRoy Grannis, Paul Naude, Scott Needham, Mikel Roberts, Jim Russi, Tom Servais, and David Tsay. Also, the AhChoy family, Georgette Austria, Jessica Trent Nichols, Milnor Pictures, Inc., and James Sartain. And let's not forget the art team: Alyssa Morris, illustrators Stacey Peterson and Michael Wang, and designer Georgia Rucker. A whopping thank you to Robert Myers for going above and beyond the call of duty with his comics-style illustrations. Check out www.RobertMyersCreates.com.**

From Sanoe to Cindy K. at Jet Set Management, my agent & friend: Thank you for all your hard work and encouragement during the hard times, and most of all thank you for being a guiding light. I love you. (That's Cindy, second from left, with Jericho Poppler, Gidget, and my mom.)